▼△▼△▼△▼△▼△▼△▼△▼△▼△▼

MARI AND THE
CURSE OF EL COCODRILO

▲▽▲▽▲▽▲▽▲▽▲▽▲▽▲▽▲

MARI
AND THE CURSE OF
EL COCODRILO

ADRIANNA CUEVAS

HARPER

An Imprint of HarperCollinsPublishers

Library of Congress Control Number: 2023934235

ISBN 978-0-06-328549-1

Typography by Corina Lupp

23 24 25 26 27 LBC 5 4 3 2 1

First Edition

To Joe.
You've always been my good luck.

ONE

THERE'S NO SUCH thing as luck.

There's just well-equipped teammates making sure a ravenous zombie doesn't chew on your brain matter for breakfast.

The New Year's Eve fireworks whistling and popping outside drown out the lasers and explosions from the game I'm playing on the computer in Papi's office.

"We have to activate the electric fences if we want to defeat the final zombie horde," my friend Keisha says in my headphones. Her voice crackles, and I adjust my earbuds.

I ignore her advice and click on my character, enabling a chainsaw attached to a shovel that I earned. My computer screen lights up with a postapocalyptic girl in dusty combat boots, a bright red scar snaking down her cheek. She runs at a small group of zombies, their bony arms reaching for her as she slices off the top half of their skulls with the chainsaw.

Keisha, Juan Carlos, and I have been trying to beat the final boss in our favorite game, *Brain Basher 3: The Munchining*, since we all got it for Christmas last week. The first levels were simple. We fought other bands of survivors, worked together to create laser fences, and gathered weapons, ammunition, and vehicles. But the final boss of the game is a lot harder—a massive stampede of zombies who come out of nowhere and rip you to shreds.

We keep dying in a pile of bloody limbs.

Juan Carlos pops into our Discord chat. "Wouldn't it be better to dig a pit and fill it with firebombs?"

Juan Carlos's character—who has long, flowy braids—swings her barbwire-wrapped bat at a zombie stumbling toward her and smashes its brains across the screen. She stands on top of the zombie's body, and I hear Juan Carlos laugh through my headphones. His character has the most kills of any of us.

Another firework whizzes outside before exploding, the high-pitched whistle and bang celebrating our near victory.

"Oye, mi cielo, tengo algo que regalarte." Abuelita taps on the doorframe behind me before shuffling farther down the hall in her house slippers.

We're so close. The meter on the final boss zombie horde is practically to zero. Soon it'll explode in a cloud of brain bits and blood.

"Almost done. Be right there," I call to Abuelita as my leg bounces in Papi's office chair. I have no idea what she has for me, but I don't think it can top beating the final boss.

"You gotta go?" Juan Carlos asks. "We've pretty much won."

I sigh. "Yeah. My abuelita wants to give me something before they do their effigy thing."

"That's the one where you throw those dolls into a fire to burn up bad luck, right?" Keisha asks. Her army sergeant character jumps on top of a burning truck and fires her grenade launcher at the stampeding zombies, her long ponytail flying behind her.

"Yep. Every year. Abuelita raided Papi's old clothes this time around to sew the dolls. At least I won't be embarrassed by all his super loud floral shirts anymore."

"Or he'll just use it as an excuse to buy new ones," Juan Carlos says. Through my headphones I can hear the fireworks exploding outside his apartment.

"Probably."

A clattering sound comes from the kitchen as Mami sets out our usual New Year's Eve treats of quesitos, pastelitos de guayaba, and empanadas de picadillo to have after midnight. My mouth starts to water as I think about sweet cream cheese and slices of guava paste wrapped in pastry crust and mini pies filled with spiced ground beef.

"I don't really care about the dolls," I say. "As long as Mocosa Mykenzye doesn't see from next door, my abuelitos can dance around the backyard with sparklers sticking out of their ears."

The breeze from the ceiling fan slithers down the back of my Houston Aeros hoodie and I shiver.

"You better hope she never finds out that you call her Booger Mykenzye. Is she still officially the worst person in sixth grade?" Keisha asks.

"She's leveled up. She took a video of Abuelito and Papi in the backyard digging the hole for our lechón on Nochebuena and posted it on Snapchat. She said they were burying a body."

"That's ridiculous," Juan Carlos says. "Lechón is the best. You don't disrespect it. Not on Christmas Eve or Tuesdays or ever."

"Yeah, tell *her* that." I click the computer mouse harder than necessary to release a razor net onto three zombies who are about to rip my arms out of their sockets.

Lechón is my favorite thing to eat. Abuelito likes to make it the traditional Cuban way, putting a whole butchered pig in a hole dug in our yard that's lined with banana leaves and topped with hot coals. It's a lot of work, but the lechón always turns out delicious, crispy skin on the outside and juicy meat on the inside.

Of course, all Mocosa Mykenzye sees is Abuelito and

Papi burying a skinned pig. I love lechón, but sometimes I wonder if it'd be easier to just grill burgers like everybody else.

"¡Oye, no comas los pastelitos antes de medianoche!" Mami shouts, loud enough for the entire neighborhood to hear, and I groan, figuring that Papi got caught trying to sneak some treats before midnight.

Maybe if my family wasn't always throwing their Cubanity out into the world for everyone to see, Mykenzye wouldn't scramble like a stumbling zombie to make fun of me at every chance. But it's no use trying to hide from her on New Year's Eve—it's always when we reach Peak Cubanity.

Abuelita grunted and groaned when she lugged a suitcase around the block because she wants to travel this year. She said that Abuelito always promises to take her to Miami, and hauling her luggage down the sidewalk guarantees that her wish will come true. I hid in my room, praying that none of the neighbors peered out the window and saw her with her huge purple bag dragging behind her.

Mami swept and mopped our whole house, except my room—because she says it's a biohazard. The bucket of dirty water sits by the front door so she can throw it out at midnight, along with all the bad luck from last year that's supposedly mixed in with the water. I can only hope Mykenzye walks by just at that moment and gets doused.

At least we won't be eating twelve grapes at midnight as fast as we can. When I almost choked last year, Papi had to do the Heimlich maneuver on me and everything. I shot a green grape straight out of my throat and into the eye of my sister, Liset.

Maybe something that's supposed to bring you good luck shouldn't also try to kill you.

Just a thought.

"¡Mari! ¡Vamos!" I hear Abuelita call from her room.

I groan again. "Y'all have to beat the zombie horde on your own," I tell my friends. "Abuelita will make me mop the whole house twelve times if I don't go now."

Clicking off *Brain Basher 3*, I head out of Papi's office and down the hall to Abuelita's bedroom. I find her sitting on her bed, her Bible on her lap. Settling next to her, I watch her trace her fingers over the names in the family tree she's written on the first page. Names like Fautina, Ladislao, and Baldomero stare back at me. I've never met any of these people. And Abuelita doesn't talk about them.

"Ay, mi cielo. Tengo un regalito para el año nuevo," Abuelita says. Placing the Bible back on her nightstand, she opens a drawer and pulls out a small book. She hands it to me and smiles, the wrinkles on her face deepening.

It's a diary. The blank pages stare at me. I have no idea how I'm supposed to fill them.

"Para apuntar tus memorias. Cada persona en nuestra

familia recibe un diario a los doce años, y ahora a ti te toca. Hay cosas que no debemos olvidar," Abuelita says, wrapping her hand over mine as I hold the diary.

I'd completely forgotten about the tradition my abuelitos started with Papi: giving a diary to each family member on their twelfth birthday. Keisha, Juan Carlos, and I had peeked at Liset's diary after she turned twelve, and it was basically a list of what she decided to wear each day. We were too bored to ever sneak a look again.

"I don't know how good writing down my memories will be if I can't read my own handwriting." I chuckle. "And I'm in middle school. There's plenty of things I'd like to forget."

Like Mocosa Mykenzye and her vomit-inducing Snapchats.

Abuelita reaches out and takes my hand. "No, mi cielo. Nuestra familia, todo lo que pasó con nosotros . . . hay que recordarlo . . ." Her voice catches in her throat. I don't know why she's talking about our family history. She may say we should remember it, but she never talks about it.

Abuelita shakes her head, as if flinging thoughts too troublesome to hold. She pulls something else out of the drawer, and my stomach drops. It's a small stuffed doll sewn from a shirt Papi wore every day when we were on vacation in Padre Island. Abuelita hands me the doll, and I grip the soft peach floral fabric.

"Con esto, ya tienes las dos cosas más importantes de la noche en tus manos. Así honramos a nuestra familia," she says.

Abuelita wants me to throw the doll into the fire at midnight, getting rid of all the bad luck from last year. But even though she says this honors our family, how much bad luck will I get if Mykenzye sees me doing this?

"Do I really have to—" I whisper, but Abuelito calls from the kitchen.

"¡Amores, todo listo!"

I sigh and tuck the doll under my arm, slipping the diary into the front pocket of my hoodie. Abuelita and I make our way down the hall, through the kitchen, and to our backyard. Everyone's already gathered at the firepit, standing around the flames like they're going to hold hands and summon a demon. The cool grass tickles my bare feet.

I glance up at Mocosa Mykenzye's house, hoping she doesn't celebrate New Year's Eve, or that she went to bed early, or that she accidentally ate her weight in creamed soup casserole and slipped into a food coma.

The air in the backyard is thick, more than the usual humidity in Port Ballí, and it smells burnt from all the fireworks people have set off. Light gray clouds of smoke drift through the sky, ghosts looking down on the grass. A breeze moves through the yard, playing with the leaves on Abuelito and Abuelita's mango and avocado trees.

Except for one mango tree in the corner. Its branches hang still, not moving from the wind. I squint at the tree and push my glasses up the bridge of my nose.

"¿Todos tienen su muñequita?" Abuelita interrupts my concentration as she passes everyone else a small fabric doll that she's sewn.

Liset waves her doll in the air and nods. I clutch my doll close to my chest, burying it in the wide sleeves of my hoodie.

"One more minute," Mami shouts, making her doll dance in front of the fire. The shadow the effigy casts on the grass is eerily alive.

I want to tell Mami to keep her voice down so she doesn't wake up Mocosa Mykenzye. I glance at the upstairs window next door, but it's still dark.

Black shadows stretch from the fire and slither slowly across the yard like snakes. I take a step closer to Liset. The dark lines weave in and out of the blades of grass as the fire flickers. The flames reach from the pit, growing closer to the doll in my arms, heat pulsing on my skin.

But there's no way they're really trying to touch me.

That would be ridiculous.

"Oye, todos listos," Abuelito says, grabbing Abuelita's hand.

Papi smiles, the fire reflecting a bright orange glow in his glasses. "We're ready," he says.

Abuelito lifts his faded plaid doll into the air, the shadow behind him a giant monster stomping across our lawn. I squint as the dark figure detaches from the effigy, stretching toward me. I scuff my feet in the dirt as my stomach rumbles, but it's not because I'm hungry.

It's more from a feeling I can't quite place, something churning in my gut like a storm in the gulf. Because no matter how many times I blink, no matter how thoroughly I wipe my glasses on my hoodie, the shadows are still there. Reaching out.

Abuelito clears his throat and counts down. "Diez, nueve, ocho, siete, seis, cinco, cuatro, tres, dos, uno . . . vete pa la porra, mala suerte."

He tosses his doll into the flames, and we stare as the fire licks at the fabric, the individual flowers brightening and then turning black as they burn. He squeezes Abuelita's hand as she cries, "¡Adiós, mala suerte!" and flings her effigy into the fire. It crackles in the flames as smoke rises above the roof of our house and swirls toward Mykenzye's window.

Abuelita leans her head on Abuelito's shoulder. She takes a deep breath as small tears form in the corner of her eyes, sparkling in the firelight. New Year's Eve is supposed to be exciting, with loud fireworks and tasty food, but some years Abuelita looks sad as she watches the fire.

I sniff and pick at a loose thread on my effigy. The air

smells like rotten fruit, which is odd because Abuelita is obsessive about picking up any mangos or avocados that fall in the yard. And this smell is different. Like when Mami keeps strawberries in the fridge too long and they start to get fuzzy. The fire calms after devouring the effigies, the shadows resting in the grass. I take a deep breath but cough on the acidic smell in the air.

Three large fireworks whizz through the air and explode above us in a rainbow of colors. The yard lights up in a white glow. I jump and almost drop the effigy.

Papi and Mami both shout, "See ya, bad luck!" and, along with Liset, toss their dolls into the fire. I wince at the shouts.

We're so *loud*.

Glancing at Mykenzye's window, I notice the striped blue curtains moving and I clench my fist around the arm of the effigy. My stomach flip-flops as the breeze swirling through the yard inches up my back and curls through my hair.

I spot Mykenzye silhouetted in the pale light coming from her bedroom. My throat tightens. Her face is just another shadow, but I can picture the smirk plastered across her thin mouth.

"Niña, hay que quemar la muñeca," Abuelita says, gesturing for me to throw my doll into the fire.

"Loquita," Liset says, her shadow stretching tight across

the yard like a creeping ghoul. "We can't eat until you toss your doll in. Let's go."

A flame erupts from the fire and licks the grass as the smoke descends on my shoulders, making me cough.

Papi joins in. "C'mon, kiddo. You know it's tradition. Don't be rude."

My eyes stay glued on the window. I see Mykenzye's phone in her hand, aimed at my backyard. I'm not letting her record this super Cuban ritual and spread it all over school like I'm some island weirdo.

I shake my head and turn away from the flickering flames reaching out for the doll in my arms. A fresh burst of sour smell erupts in the yard and hits my nose. I gasp as my throat closes. Suddenly the wriggling shadows in the grass all straighten and start slithering wildly toward me. The fire crackles and pops, sending sparks into the air. They sail up, and the wind shoots them in my direction while a high-pitched howl swirls in my ears.

Before I can spot the source of the sound, my feet catch under me and I tumble to the ground. Something tugs on my ankle as I try to get back up. Clawing at the grass, I dig my elbows in the dirt, trying to stand.

"Mi cielo, ¿estás bien?" Abuelita asks as she watches me writhe in the grass like I'm possessed.

I barely hear her, my heartbeat thudding loudly in my ears as I wonder what in the world is happening. I feel the pull on my foot again, like fingers digging into my skin. My ankle is going to snap.

"I . . . I don't know," I stammer. But I can't get any more words out.

The flames in the firepit inch closer to my leg, and sharp heat licks my bare heel. I look across the yard and spot the mango tree that was so strangely still earlier. Its leaves are flailing, as if something invisible is shaking the trunk. A series of fireworks burst in the sky, sounding like breaking bones.

"Oh my god, loquita! What are you doing?" Liset asks, rolling her eyes.

She grabs my arm and yanks me up, away from the fire. I look back at the pit, and the flames grow longer, fiery fingers grasping for me.

"I . . . I'm not sure," I say, sweat dripping down my forehead as my stomach churns in confusion. "I tripped."

I can't tell them about the invisible pull on my foot or the shadows reaching for me. There's no way they would believe me. *I* don't even believe me.

I scan the yard. Abuelito is obsessed with keeping it in perfect condition, and I don't see any rocks or roots that might've made me fall.

"You okay there, kiddo?" Papi asks, patting me on the back.

I don't even want to turn and see Mocosa Mykenzye's

window. I don't want to know if she caught my ridiculous performance on her phone. I squint as the shadows cast by my abuelitos' legs break off and slither through the yard toward me, long black figures moving slowly between the blades of grass, reaching to wrap around my ankles.

"Do you see that?" I ask, holding out a shaking finger at the moving shapes in the yard.

Papi shrugs and shakes his head. "What are you talking about there, kiddo?"

"Do we need to make an eye appointment for you?" Mami asks.

I shake my head and rub my eyes under my glasses. "I'm going inside," I grumble.

I've been playing *Brain Basher 3* too much. It's making me see things. And feel them too.

That has to be it.

The cold breeze from the yard follows me into the house, climbing up the back of my hoodie and blowing on my neck, making me shiver.

I pass the kitchen table, piled high with quesitos, pastelitos, and empanadas, but my stomach rolls and acid rises in my throat.

When I get to my room, I pull the effigy from my hoodie and throw it on my bed. The diary Abuelita gave me tumbles out of my pocket too and lands on my foot, the hard spine stinging my toes. I just want this stupid holiday to be over.

This has never happened before. We toss the effigies into the fire and eat. No creepy shadows, no out-of-control fire, no invisible force grabbing me and knocking me to the ground.

I don't know what made this year different, or how I could have imagined all that, even if it's the only explanation I've got.

I punch my pillow and flop onto my bed. I'm certain Mykenzye will post the video she took of me so everyone will see it before we go back to school after winter break. All because my family insists on parading our Cubanity around all the time.

More fireworks explode outside, high-pitched screams flying through the air.

As I look at the effigy upside down next to my pillow, one of the flowers on the fabric stretches across the head, the petals sharpening into a toothy grin.

I narrow my eyes and poke the effigy in its stuffed belly with my finger. The moment I touch the fabric, a sharp pain erupts on my forearm.

I push the sleeve of my hoodie up as a thick black splotch grows across my skin. I slap my arm, trying to brush it off, but nothing happens. The mark keeps growing, looking like the shadows that crept out from the fire. I start to yell for help, but my throat closes up, the sickening sweet smell from the backyard flooding my nostrils again.

My breath catches in my throat as I flex my fingers. I squint at my forearm and the dark mark stomping across my skin like a crocodile.

My heart beats in my ears, and I shake my head.

I know my super Cuban family. I know my stupid neighbor.

But I have no idea what this is.

TWO

FORGET BEATING THE zombie horde in *Brain Basher* 3. I have a new mission: making sure no one in my family sees the black splotch on my forearm.

I woke up on New Year's Day, and the crocodile-shaped mark was still crawling across my arm. I tried to wash it off, scrubbing it until my skin was red, but it won't go away.

I spent the last two days tugging on the sleeves of my hoodies, making sure no one sees it, especially not Abuelita or Mami. They'd slather my skin with Vivaporu while muttering "sana, sana, colita de rana." But this means wearing long sleeves all the time, even though Port Ballí doesn't get that cool in the winter.

I start sweating immediately whenever I put on a hoodie or a long-sleeve shirt. Mami's gonna have to buy me a case of extra-strength deodorant at the grocery store.

Today the challenge is even more complicated. It's the first day back from winter break, so I also have to make sure no one at school sees the mark. And definitely not Mocosa Mykenzye.

Which is why I'm in the bathroom rummaging through all of Liset's lotions and makeup to find anything that might cover it up.

"Mari, hurry up!" Liset yells as she bangs on the door. "You're taking way longer than your usual three minutes, and I have to pee."

"Be right out," I say, knocking over Liset's powder, which I was dabbing over the thick black stain on my arm. It clatters on the bathroom floor and spews a cloud of light brown dust everywhere.

Yanking the sleeves of my Port Ballí Community College hoodie down to my wrists, I clean up the powder as best I can with my bath towel, knowing Abuelita will make me soak it in Fabuloso when she sees the stain.

I'm stuffing the towel into the laundry hamper when my phone buzzes in my pocket. I glance at the text message.

Do you have my copy of Red Panda and Moon Bear or does Juan Carlos? Syed wants to read it.

I tuck my phone into my hoodie after reading Keisha's text. We've been best friends since kindergarten, when we both sat outside the school health office along with Juan Carlos as the nurse went over the disastrous results of our vision tests. Like, we could've won an award for the worst reading of the eye chart. I think I even invented some new letters. All three of us had to get glasses after that, but I dubbed us Los Super Ojos and told Keisha and Juan Carlos that our glasses gave us superpowers. We've been best friends ever since.

Syed, a boy from Keisha's fencing team, doesn't wear glasses. And he's definitely not part of Los Super Ojos. He's more like Manolito, Liset's first boyfriend in eighth grade. All of a sudden she was hanging out with him constantly instead of with her best friend, Ciara. They had a huge argument about it on our front lawn as Ciara blamed Liset for abandoning her.

I don't want to argue with Keisha on our front lawn.

I don't want to argue with Keisha period.

I sit on the edge of the bathtub and lift the leg of my jeans. My foot is still sore from falling next to the firepit on New Year's Eve, and I slather a thick layer of Vivaporu on my ankle, figuring maybe Abuelita's cure will help.

I can't figure out what happened that night. One minute I'm checking to make sure Mocosa Mykenzye isn't spying on me, the next minute something is dragging me across the ground toward the fire. When I close my eyes, I can still see the shadows creeping across the yard. Even though I tried to convince myself that my mind was just making all those things up, the permanent stain on my forearm is definitely real.

And I don't know what to do about it.

I buried the effigy under a pile of clothes, but every morning, it's lying right on top of my dirty jeans and T-shirts. I keep waking up at night, expecting to catch it crawling over the mountain of laundry, its flowery teeth bared as it skitters toward my bed.

I've got it. It's in my room . . . somewhere. I text back.

Juan Carlos jumps into our never-ending text thread. It's too early, Super Ojos. Even hyper dolphins aren't chatting this early. . .

Did you find it yet? Keisha asks. I wanna give it to Syed at practice today.

. . .She'd probably have better luck if you'd quit texting herdfgs

I squint at Juan Carlos's text on my phone. Juanito? You ok?

I put the Vivaporu back in the medicine cabinet and open the door to see Liset's raised eyebrows and tapping foot.

"About time," she says as I head to the living room. Liset goes to Port Ballí High School, which starts a full hour after my school. So she's still comfy in her blue llama-print pajamas, her dark brown hair piled on top of her head in a messy bun.

Juan Carlos finally texts back. Don't text and skateboard, Super Ojos. Almost hit a tree.

Staring at my phone, I bump into Papi standing in the

living room. "You're gonna be late, kiddo," he says, taking a long sip of coffee and nudging me with his elbow. I look up and see his eyes glued to the TV along with Abuelito and Abuelita as it blares the news.

"What's going on?" I ask.

Abuelito shakes his head as he sits on the couch. "Que Dios les cuide."

A reporter shows two kids my age holding hands and sitting in the dirt, surrounded by men dressed in dark green.

"They're talking about some unaccompanied minors that came to Texas," Papi says.

"What's an unaccompanied minor?"

"They came to the US by themselves. Without any adults."

I can't imagine being brave enough to do that. I freak out when I get separated from Mami in the grocery store. Never mind coming to an entirely new country.

"Ay, pobrecitos," Abuelita murmurs as she gets up from the couch and heads to the kitchen. I notice her wiping the corners of her eyes with the back of her hand.

"Is Abuelita okay?" I ask Papi.

He gives me a small smile. "News like this brings up hard memories. You know Abuelo and Abuela came by themselves to the US. A lot of our family did. But not everyone made it safely."

I look from Papi to Abuelito. Smoothing his hand over the embroidery of his guayabera, Abuelito sighs. "Su primita Andaluz. Que en paz descanse."

My fingers reach into the sleeve of my hoodie and scratch the mark on my arm. "Her cousin?"

Papi nods and takes another sip of his coffee. "Andaluz drowned trying to cross the Florida Straits between Cuba and the US."

I swallow hard. I've never heard this story before. I wonder if Andaluz is one of the names Abuelita has listed in her Bible. My forearm tingles as I scratch it, and I tug on the sleeve of my hoodie. I shake my hand, trying to get rid of the feeling.

"How old was she? When did she try to come over here? Why did she come by herself?" I ask as the mark on my arm heats up. I must've scratched it too hard.

"That story is for another day; you're running late. You'd better get going," Papi says before I can ask him anything else.

Abuelito rubs his eyes and ignores my questions too.

I grab my backpack from the side of the couch where I threw it last night after I packed it for school, and I start to head out the door. But Abuelita calls from the kitchen, "Niña, hay que desayunar."

"I'll have breakfast at school," I tell her.

Abuelita peeks in from the kitchen and shakes her head,

planting her hands on her hips. She takes a deep breath, swallowing down what she saw on the news to focus on my less-than-amazing dietary habits. "¿Esa basura? No."

"It's not garbage."

Liset snickers as she comes down the hallway. "The breakfast burritos could survive an atomic explosion," she says under her breath.

"Maricela Yanet Feijoo. You. Eat. Breakfast," Abuelita insists, ushering me into the kitchen. She wraps a slice of Cuban bread slathered with guava jelly and cream cheese in a paper towel and thrusts it at me.

Papi chuckles as he opens a package of bacon to add to a hot frying pan on the stove. "Ouch. Full name. And English. There's no winning this battle, kiddo."

Abuelita clicks her tongue and snaps a towel at Papi. The glint in her eyes makes it obvious she isn't really mad.

I accept defeat and grab the sandwich.

"You forgetting something?" Liset asks, not bothering to look up, her eyes glued to her phone.

I stop in my tracks and raise an eyebrow at her. Liset sets her phone down on the kitchen counter and lifts her arms, mimicking holding a violin and bow.

Smacking my forehead with my hand, I toss the sandwich on the counter and run back to my room to grab my violin case. I spot the diary Abuelita gave me and, next to it, the book Keisha wanted and shove them into my backpack.

At least I can list my family's Peak Cubanity in the diary when I get bored in class. And maybe Keisha will stop talking about Syed once I give her the book.

Slinging my case over my shoulder, I hurry down the hallway, wanting to get outside before Liset or Abuelita tells me I should brush my hair or that my navy T-shirt doesn't match my jeans.

"¡Ponte un suéter!" Abuelita calls from the kitchen. "Está chiflando el mono afuera."

Note for the diary: instead of just saying "It's cold outside," Abuelita insists on saying "The monkey is whistling."

"Run, kiddo. Run." Papi winks at me as he takes another swig of his coffee and flips the strips of crackling bacon in the pan.

"Gotta go! Can't be late!" I shout, grabbing my sandwich and not bothering to put on a sweater like Abuelita told me. I'm already wearing a long-sleeve hoodie. There's not enough deodorant in the world for a sweater on top of a hoodie in Texas.

My shoes squeak on the floor as I start to race out of the kitchen. But the rubber on the bottom of my shoes sticks to the tile. I jerk my foot, but it stays glued to the floor.

"So are you going or not?" Liset stares at me and raises her eyebrow.

"I . . . um." I don't know what to say. Did Abuelita use Fabuloso mixed with superglue to clean the kitchen? I feel a familiar pressure again on my ankle, and goose bumps raise up and down my arms. I yank my foot again, but nothing happens.

That's when I feel the pull, the same fiery fingers that wrapped around my ankle on New Year's Eve.

I look behind me, and the flames under the skillet Papi's using grow and lick the sides of the pan. A deep growl fills the kitchen, tumbling against the cabinets and rolling up my legs, making my spine shake.

Mine.

I look from Liset to Abuelita and Papi to see if they heard the voice too, but they're all staring at me. My stomach flip-flops as the mark on my arm starts to tingle again, a little at first, and then more and more, until it feels like someone is holding a match to my skin. I wince and wrap my hand around the sleeve of my hoodie. My backpack straps press into my shoulders, the contents inside squirming and poking me in the spine.

I feel pressure on my body, this time not just on my ankle. Invisible hands push my shoulders back toward the fire coming from the stove burner. My palms sweat and my back shakes as I try to break free.

"Kiddo, what the frijoles you doing? Menea el esqueleto or you're really going to be late," Papi says, telling me to hurry up. He gives me a playful shove, and I feel my feet release from the floor.

I stumble forward and take a deep breath, my shoulders quivering.

"Loquita," Liset says, winking at me.

I shrug off her comment, but an uneasy feeling grows in my stomach. I wiggle my fingers as the burning feeling on my arm fades.

Hearing the school bus brakes squeak outside, Abuelita ushers me out the front door. I push up my glasses on the bridge of my nose and peek at the bottoms of my shoes. There's nothing there that could've cemented me to the kitchen floor.

Yet another thing I can't explain. That list is getting longer than the list of Peak Cubanity I was planning to make in the diary.

"Que tengas buen día, mi vida," Abuelito says from his usual perch on the plastic folding chair on the front porch. He's reading the newspaper and humming his favorite song, a slow Cuban ballad. Three laughing gulls circle near our porch, waiting for Abuelito to toss bits of Cuban bread at them.

"I will, Abuelito," I say, my voice slightly quivering as I try to calm down. I clench my fists to cover up how much I'm still shaking over what happened in the kitchen. "Mariachi practice starts again today."

Abuelito chuckles and shakes his head as the wind off

the gulf snaps the pages of his newspaper. "Una cubana tocando mariachi. Qué cosa."

"It's not weird for a Cuban to play mariachi," I call to him as I get on the bus. My bag feels hot against my back as I slump in my seat. Slipping it off my shoulders, I pull out my new diary, and at the bottom of the bag I find a pen I gnawed on during a science test.

Turning to a clean page, I write January 3 at the top. For the moment, I change my plan to use Abuelita's diary to track all my family's ridiculous traditions. It's been three days since New Year's Eve, and the weirdness is only increasing. Instead, I make a list of everything that's happened that I can't explain: the stretching shadows, the pull on my foot in front of the fire, the mark on my arm, the effigy constantly reappearing in my room, and my feet sticking to the kitchen floor.

I don't know what's going on, but I'm going to figure it out.

My pen quivers in my hand and I bite my lip.

I know this isn't how Abuelita said I should use the diary. And she would've clicked her tongue disapprovingly at my original plan to track all our Peak Cubanity. She wanted me to write about our family and our history. But even though we celebrate all our Cuban traditions, it's not like we've ever actually talked about our family's history.

Like this morning when I asked questions about Andaluz, no one would even answer me.

I don't understand why they won't talk about their life or their family in Cuba, especially when they make such a big deal about being Cuban here. All I've got are bits and pieces, and maybe that's what I should actually use the diary for—keeping all the different puzzle pieces until I can make a complete picture of our family's story.

I quickly scrawl at the bottom of the page, "Abuelita's cousin Andaluz died when she was trying to cross the Florida Straits from Cuba to the United States. I don't know more. She never talks about her."

I scan my words and read them over again.

The school bus hits a hole in the pavement and jerks. I bounce in my seat and watch as the letters sink into the paper and swirl in small, inky whirlpools, as if someone dropped water on the page.

THREE

I GET OFF the bus, the humid Port Ballí air fogging up my glasses. I pushed my diary to the bottom of my backpack, but I'm still wondering why the only things that bled were the inked letters on the last thing I wrote. I cleaned my glasses three times with the edge of my hoodie, and the letters still looked fuzzy on the page.

I'm inspecting the page when Juan Carlos runs up to me, his always-bruised knuckles tapping the top of the skateboard in his hands. There's a little bit of dirt on his black shirt and jeans, probably from his battle with a tree this morning. Juan Carlos's mom is an eighth-grade science teacher, so he always gets to school earlier than everyone else and rides around the neighborhood before the first bell rings. All the roads and sidewalks in Port Ballí are built over sand, so the unstable, cracked asphalt guarantees that his knees are constantly scabbed and his hands are forever scratched.

Abuelita would cover him completely in Vivaporu.

"Hey, did you know that clown fish can change sex? Like from male to female and female to male?" he asks, tucking his skateboard under his arm. He flips his shaggy black hair out of his eyes and pushes his red-framed glasses up the bridge of his nose with his finger.

"Some people just say good morning, Juanito." I roll my fingers and try to shake off the weirdness of the kitchen and the bus this morning. I scuff the soles of my shoes on the sidewalk as the gulf wind slaps my ponytail in my face.

I hike the strap of my violin case on my shoulder and walk up the steps to school with Juan Carlos. "They should let you lead all the tours at the wildlife center," I tell him.

Juan Carlos volunteers at the Port Ballí Wildlife Center and Rescue. He mostly cleans up after sea turtles, fish, and armies of seabirds, which means he's normally elbow-deep in poop.

I don't think Abuelita's Vivaporu could help with that. Even it has its limits.

Juan Carlos holds the door open for me, and we walk into school dodging snotty kindergartners and tripping over distracted first graders. Even though we're in sixth grade, Port Ballí is small enough that kindergarten through eighth grade are all in the same building. It's only the high schoolers who have their own booger-free space.

"Is it too early to start a 'days until summer' countdown?"

Juan Carlos asks. "At least we're starting back on a Thursday. I think I can survive two days. Maybe."

I hear a shrill giggle behind me and instantly lower my head, hugging my violin case to my chest.

"Good morning, Fee-Joe," a high-pitched voice sings over the rumble of kids in the hallway. "Did your family have a good Christmas? I mean, do they celebrate Christmas in Mexico?"

Mocosa Mykenzye saunters toward us, the smirk plastered on her pale face revealing how much her incisors look like snake fangs.

I bite my lip and glance pleadingly at Juan Carlos, my stomach rumbling as my palms sweat.

It doesn't matter how many times I tell Mykenzye that my last name is pronounced "fay-ho," she delights in destroying every syllable of it while asking ignorant questions. She posted the New Year's Eve video of me on Snapchat, and it seems like most of the school watched it, half of them wondering what kind of psycho ritual my family was conducting in our backyard.

"She's not Mexican, genius," Juan Carlos says, rolling his eyes in Mykenzye's direction. She doesn't respond and keeps strolling down the hallway, showing her phone to the person next to her. They both look at me and laugh.

Juan Carlos turns to me. "Just ignore her."

I sigh. "That's a little hard. She's nonstop."

"Have you told Mr. Nguyen or any of the other teachers?"

"What's the point?" I ask, shrugging. "If I tell them she says my name wrong, or makes comments about the food my family eats, or posts weird videos of me, it doesn't sound like she's doing anything so terrible. It's the fact that everything she does just piles one on top of the other."

Juan Carlos gives me a weak smile and puts his hand on my shoulder. "Want me to put a squid in her hair? You know I can get one."

I shake my head and laugh. "No. That's okay."

My stomach starts to settle as I watch Mykenzye walk away from us, her green-tinged blond hair swinging like a lizard's tail. Juan Carlos shoves his skateboard into the strap on his backpack and shrugs.

"On to better things than Mocosa Mykenzye. When's your mariachi tryout?"

I tuck a frizzy strand of hair behind my ear as a freckled second grader runs down the hall dangling a squirming worm between his fingers. "Three weeks. We start practice again today."

Three days a week after school, the sixth graders who want to play mariachi in seventh and eighth grade have practice. I can't wait to dive back into the noise of violins, trumpets, and guitars after winter break. It's always a good distraction from whichever way Mocosa Mykenzye decides to wriggle under my skin that day like a maggot.

"Ugh. Move, please," a voice mumbles behind us.

I turn and see Keisha pick up a first grader attempting to tie his shoe for the fifth time and move him out of her way. She runs up to us, hiking a long athletic bag on her shoulder. "You think I could fit him in my fencing bag?"

I chuckle. "Why in the world would you want to do that?"

Keisha shrugs and wrinkles her nose, bobbing her purple glasses up and down. "I don't know. First graders make good sparring dummies. They're squishy."

Juan Carlos gives Keisha a high five. "Did that Houston coach ever come see you over break?"

Keisha shakes her head. "Not yet. He'll be at my tournament in a week or so." Gripping her fencing bag tighter, she nods. "I'll be ready."

I slap her on the back. It's her goal to make it into the Junior Olympics, and being on the Houston Daggers elite team is a step toward that.

Juan Carlos turns to Keisha. "Remember—stab, stab, stab. Simple."

"There's a little more to it than that," Keisha says, lunging toward Juan Carlos and poking him in the stomach with her index finger. "Syed's been helping me practice my flèche."

Resisting the urge to roll my eyes at the mention of Syed, I pull *Red Panda and Moon Bear* out of my backpack and thrust it at Keisha.

The school bell erupts over the noise in the hallway, and I jump as Keisha takes the book. I'm still on edge from this morning.

We start to walk down the hallway when Juan Carlos leans in and whispers, "Hey, no judgment here, but aren't you a little old to bring a doll to school?"

I look at Juan Carlos, and he juts his chin at my backpack. As I slide it off my shoulder, my eyes widen as Abuelita's effigy sticks halfway out of my bag, like it's trying to free itself and crawl up the back of my neck.

"What the frijoles?" I mutter. I didn't see it when I got my diary out of my bag on the bus or when I took out Keisha's book. Did Liset put it in there as a joke? Did it crawl from my pile of dirty clothes and into my backpack? Dolls can't do that, right?

Mykenzye has shown that New Year's Eve video to everyone in school. I don't need her to catch me with a doll in the middle of the hallway. My family has already embarrassed me enough.

Keisha pulls the doll out of my bag, her fingers wrapping around a flowery arm, and she immediately gasps. She drops it to the scratched tile floor and clutches her hand.

"Ow! It stung me! What kind of fabric is on that thing?"

I bend down and pick the doll off the floor, glancing at Keisha's arm. I blink as a black splotch in the shape of a crocodile appears on her dark brown skin just above her wrist.

I think I might throw up.

"Did your abuela make that?" Juan Carlos asks, reaching for the doll. I clutch it to my chest, not wanting him to touch it too.

"Yeah, it's from New Year's Eve," I tell them, shoving the effigy into my backpack. "I have no idea how it got in there. It's so weird."

If both Keisha and I got a mark right after touching the effigy Abuelita made, something has to be wrong with it. But what do the marks mean?

I look from Juan Carlos to Keisha. She hasn't noticed the small black mark on her skin yet. I fight the urge to inspect every inch of fabric on the doll, because I don't want Mocosa Mykenzye seeing me holding a toy in the middle of the hallway. I shove it back into my bag instead.

Just as the tardy bell rings, we race into our first period, Mr. Nguyen's math class. I plop down in my seat between Keisha and Juan Carlos as our teacher announces a "welcome back to school" quiz over fractions.

I groan. Mr. Nguyen clearly has a different idea of "welcome" than I do.

Juan Carlos lays his head on his desk, but Keisha smiles and cracks her knuckles.

Mr. Nguyen passes out the quizzes, walking up and down each aisle. The class hushes as heads bow over papers and pencils scribble. The wind outside picks up and taps a long oak branch against the classroom window.

I look over my quiz and breathe a sigh of relief. I'm pretty sure I can multiply these fractions. I start to write my answer to the first question when the tip of my pencil snaps off on my paper, leaving a dark gray slash.

I look at the window as I hop up to sharpen my pencil, and I spot five thick moths beating their wings against the glass. Weird. I thought those only came out at night around streetlights.

Returning to my seat, I try to write, but the sharp tip of my pencil snaps off again, flies across the aisle, and smacks Juan Carlos in the cheek.

He looks at me and raises his eyebrow.

I mouth "sorry" and examine my pencil. This has to be one of those pencils from the dollar store that Mami buys in bulk for her students—they never work. But before I can find a way to fix my pencil situation, the sound of water fills the classroom.

Drip

Drip

Drip

I glance around, trying to find the source. There aren't

any faucets in Mr. Nguyen's classroom. Where is that noise coming from?

No one else has noticed the sound either. They're all focused on the quiz, like I should be. I check out the window, looking for rain, but all I see is more moths beating against the glass with their spotted brown wings.

Reaching into my bag, I pull out my pencil case. It feels softer in my hands than usual, and when I unzip it, a horde of wriggling black worms crawl out onto my fingers. I scream, dropping my pencil case to the floor.

Everyone in class stares at me.

"Mari, is everything all right?" Mr. Nguyen asks, standing up from his desk.

I look down at the case. Eight yellow pencils lay scattered across the floor.

"Um, yes sir. I, uh . . . it's nothing," I stammer, taking off my glasses and cleaning them on the edge of my hoodie.

"You are so weird," I hear Mykenzye whisper behind me, making my cheeks flush.

I collect my pencils and take a deep breath, trying to concentrate on my quiz, but I can't get the image of the worms out of my mind or the sound of water out of my ears.

Drip

Drip

Drip

Looking over the first question again, I figure out the answer and start to write "*three-fifths*" on my paper. The tip of my new pencil snaps off again, as if someone is flicking the end of it every time I start to write.

All of a sudden, the rhythm of the drips increases, a steady flow like the rush of a creek. I scan the room, but every student is hunched over their quiz, scribbling away. And it's still a bright day, sunlight peeking in through the wings of the moths that have gathered on the window glass.

The flow of water gets louder now, thundering waves crashing on a beach. I bring my hands to my ears and squeeze my eyes shut. My stomach rolls, and I think I might throw up all over my quiz.

And then, silence.

The moths fly away from the window as Mr. Nguyen announces it's time to turn in our quizzes. I stare at my blank paper, acid rising in my throat. I can picture Mami's arched eyebrow and hear the click of her tongue as I show her my failing grade.

The bell rings, and we trudge to our next class. I keep my eyes on the pipes hanging from the ceiling in our old school building, wondering if they're going to burst any second, flooding the hallways.

When we arrive in our social studies class, our teacher, Ms. Faruqi, looks more excited than I've ever seen her.

It's never good when teachers are excited.

She clears her throat, and I prepare for the worst.

"Good morning, class. Today, I get to tell you about my favorite project," she announces. "Every year, the sixth grade has a world fair, where each student presents information about a country they've chosen. It can be any country you want. In March, we'll have a showcase in the cafeteria. I can't wait to see what you all come up with. We've had some absolutely wonderful projects in years past."

Mykenzye mutters behind me, "Bet that one messes up and lets it slip that her family's here illegally from Mexico."

I clench the sides of my desk. I want to scream that my family is from Cuba, but I know it's pointless. For as obviously as my family makes their Cubanity known, Mykenzye just doesn't care. We're all the same to her. *And* she's ignorant enough to treat being undocumented like an insult, which is stupid.

I look over at Keisha and watch her scratch her arm, just above her wrist. Her fingers push the sleeves of her T-shirt up, and she spots the black mark, a long crocodile crawling up her arm, exactly like mine. Keisha's eyebrows raise as she rubs her thumb over the mark again and again.

I've got bigger problems than Mykenzye now.

FOUR

IT'S BEEN A busier first day back at school than I
wanted: avoiding Mykenzye and her comments, dealing
with constantly breaking pencils and ghost worms, hearing
weird dripping noises everywhere, and, most of all, worrying about the mark on my skin and Keisha's.

I breathe a sigh of relief when I walk into the music
room after school, but it catches in my throat and I cough.
There's no way that my disastrous day isn't connected to
the mark on my arm. And now that my best friend has the
same mark, what does that mean for her?

For the moment, I've convinced Keisha that it might be
a late-blooming bruise from fencing practice. She almost
didn't believe me, declaring, "I'm too good to get hit that
hard." But what will she think when the "bruise" doesn't
heal? I need to get answers for the both of us before she
becomes suspicious.

I find my seat and get my instrument ready, rubbing

rosin on the strings of my bow and placing my chin pad on the body of my violin.

"Ready for the audition?" asks Ines, another sixth grader, as she sits down next to me and taps her foot repeatedly on the chair leg. Her hair is in two long black braids down her back, and a small red flower sits at the end of each braid.

I wish I could do my hair like that, but it would probably look like two dying snakes shedding their skin.

"I hope so," I confess. "But we've still got a couple weeks. And I've been practicing."

Ines smiles. "Me too. My mom and abuela have been helping me. They were both in mariachi when they were in school too." She takes out her violin bow and twists the knob at the end to tighten the hairs. "Was your family in mariachi?"

I shake my head. "No. They don't really know anything about it. We're Cuban. I just like the music."

I discovered mariachi music listening to the radio with Abuelito on our front porch when I was eight. I'd convinced him to listen to something other than Cuban music and found a station where a man named Vicente Fernandez sang, his voice full of passion and strength. A chorus of violins and guitars tumbled out of the speakers and filled my ears. I begged Mami and Papi to let me take violin lessons the very next day. I haven't stopped playing since, something that's obvious from the calluses on the fingers of my left hand. And the fact that I tap out rhythms on my thigh all the time.

"Yeah, me too," Ines says, running her bow slowly across her violin and twisting the silver pegs near her chin to fine-tune the strings.

I do the same, but the wooden pegs on the neck of my violin keep slipping, making the strings lie loose and flat. I grab some wax from my violin case and apply it to the pegs so they'll hold the strings tighter. Mr. Quintera, the mariachi director for the seventh and eighth grade, calls us to attention and explains the audition process that will take place in a few weeks.

"Each student will play a piece you've prepared as well as one piece that I will give you," he says. "We'll spend our practice time together working on the piece we will all play."

My stomach rumbles, and I take a deep breath. I want to focus on practicing my individual piece, not Ms. Faruqi's stupid world fair project. Or pencils sabotaging my schoolwork. Or weird noises.

Or the marks on my arm and Keisha's.

I wipe my hands on my jeans. I place my sheet music on the metal stand in front of me, but the top of the black stand lowers with a thud. I grab the edges of the top and raise it again, but it sinks slowly, like some invisible weight is pushing it down.

Drip

Drip

Drip

My skin crawls. There it is again. The water.

I snap my head from side to side, searching the classroom, checking again to see if anyone else hears the noise. But all the students are focused on their own music and instruments. No one seems to notice the sound of a faucet running.

"Here, you can share with me," Ines says, scooting her stand closer to me. "That one seems messed up."

Mr. Quintera snaps his fingers and explains the song we're all going to play, "México Lindo y Querido."

Ines flips her music to the right page as everyone prepares their instruments. Just as Mr. Quintera begins the song and the class starts to play, I look at the sheet music and squint. The notes sway and bounce across the page, twisting and changing position. I squeeze my eyes shut and shake my head. I'd cleaned my glasses before class, like always, so why does the sheet music look like a splatter of paint drops?

I glance at Ines to see if she's noticed, but she's playing perfectly as usual, following the music with no problems.

Mr. Quintera tilts his head to the side when he sees I'm not playing. I quickly raise my violin to my shoulder and tuck it under my chin.

Taking a deep breath, I watch Ines for a moment and figure out where the class is in the song. I'd practiced "México Lindo y Querido" enough over winter break, even giving my parents and abuelitos mini concerts in the living room, so I've got the song memorized.

Calming myself down with another deep breath, I raise my bow to join the class in the piece. But as I look down the neck of the violin, something's wrong.

The wooden peg holding the D string begins to turn. Instead of loosening, the way it did at the beginning of practice, it's tightening the string, winding harder and harder around the peg, as if turned by an invisible hand.

"What the frijoles?" I mumble. Violin pegs don't just tighten on their own.

The mark on my arm stings, burning as if it's on fire. I wince and drop my bow onto the D string. It snaps and flies loose from the peg, whipping through the air and snapping against the lens of my glasses.

Gasping, I lower my violin and press my hand to my cheek. Good thing my glasses protected my eyes, or I'd be a pirate for Halloween from now until forever.

Ines keeps playing with the class but whispers to me, "You okay?"

My heart pounds in my ears. I know violins shouldn't take on a life of their own. I know notes on sheet music don't just swirl and move for no reason. I know the dripping sound I keep hearing isn't because the building for Port Ballí Primary School is probably a thousand years old.

"I . . . I have to go," I say, quickly packing up my instrument and rushing out of the room before Mr. Quintera can say anything.

Hurrying to the bathroom to check my glasses, I feel my backpack grow heavier and heavier. I slip it off my shoulders and open it, wondering what could weigh so much. All I see at the bottom, between my diary and crumpled notebooks, is the effigy, the smirk across its face now joined by a moldy black splotch growing like a tentacled monster on the center of its belly.

FIVE

I LOOK AT myself in the school bathroom mirror and notice a small scratch running along the left lens of my glasses, thankful that no one is in here with me to witness my freak-out. Mami's gonna be more annoyed than a lobster in a boiling pot when she sees it. She already clicks her tongue whenever I can't find my glasses in my room. Which is usually at least once a week.

But I'd rather picture Mami's arched eyebrow and her chin jutting out in the direction of my scratched lens than relive whatever just happened at mariachi practice. My spine shakes when I picture the scrambled sheet music and whipping violin strings.

And I absolutely don't want to think about the effigy sitting at the bottom of my backpack. Eyeing the trash can in the corner of the bathroom, I resist the urge to dump the doll in there. I don't want to touch it or look at it. Who knows what would happen?

I take my glasses off and set them on the side of the sink. Turning on the faucet, I splash my face with cold water. My cheeks still burn and my arm aches where the black splotch sits sunken into my skin like a bruise that never fades.

I cram my glasses back on my face and run my fingers under the water coming out of the faucet.

It's burning hot.

The mirror above the sink fogs up, and I gasp as letters begin to appear on the glass, as if written by an invisible hand.

GOOD . . . LUCK . . . MARI

Hot bile rises in my throat. How is this happening?

I reach to wipe the mirror with my hand, but the glass turns black. A thick shadow creeps along the wall and covers the mirror. Just as I jerk my hand away from it, water explodes from the sink, drenching the mirror and erasing the writing. The shadow along the wall pulls away and moves to cover the ceiling tiles above me. I jump back and slip in a puddle, falling down.

My back crashes into the door of one of the stalls, banging it open. I try to get up, but my foot slides across the tile as my jeans get soaked. That's when I hear the giggle.

It echoes in the bathroom, skittering off the tiles like a

horde of bugs. The high-pitched whine crawls into my ears, and I shiver.

The lights above me flicker with a snap and pop.

The snicker erupts again, gliding over the puddles on the floor. The stall door next to me slams open, a sharp crack making me jump. My mouth drops open as a dark head peeks out, a bony, white-knuckled hand gripping the partition one finger at a time.

Black eyes stare at me, and thin lips stretch in a smirk.

As my shoes slip in the water, I push my feet across the floor, trying to move away from the creature coming out of the stall. I shove myself back until I hit the far wall of the bathroom.

A girl in a sopping-wet blue dress laughs, but her face is stone, glaring at me as water drips down her gray skin. The black mark on my arm pulses, a thousand needles pricking my skin.

Swallowing hard, I clench my fists and stammer, "What . . . who are you?"

The girl's charcoal eyes dart to my arm and then to my bag sitting on the edge of the sink. "What? No 'thank you'?" she says, her voice falling flat in the usually echoing bathroom as she stares me down.

I avert my eyes from her gaze, her black eyes narrowing at me. Staring at the ceiling, I spot a shadow creeping around the bathroom lights and slithering down to the sink. A squelching sound comes from the faucet, and a fat, dark green lizard squirms out of the spout and crawls across the edge of the sink toward my backpack and violin case. The pipes in the bathroom gurgle and whine as two more slimy lizards squish their way out of the faucet.

I wrap my arms around my legs and shake my head, wondering if any of this is real. The shadow pushes the lizards toward my backpack, but before I can react, the puddle next to me erupts in a wave, its invisible, watery hand shoving the lizards onto the floor, across the tile, and up into a toilet. The shadow retreats again, resting on the wall above the stall, pulsing and waiting.

The girl smirks, her thin, dark lips stretching. "Nice try, but you can't beat me."

"I—I wasn't trying to," I stammer, my voice catching in my throat.

Rolling her black eyes, the girl waves a dismissive hand toward the shadow on the wall. "Not you. Him."

The shadow snakes across the ceiling above me and down the wall toward the sink where my backpack sits, creeping closer and closer. The girl takes her foot and dips it into the puddle on the floor. The water swirls, growing higher and higher in a column. I blink as seaweed and small fish appear. The girl wiggles her fingers, and the water slams into the sink next to my backpack.

A shriek rips through the bathroom, and for just a

moment I spot the outline of a person on the wall before the shadow completely vanishes.

The girl brushes her hands together and rolls her shoulders. "Well, now that he's gone and we're alone, I can tell you: you're a complete mess."

My heartbeat in my throat threatens to choke me, but I manage to blurt out, "What's happening? Did . . . did you write that message on the mirror?"

The girl hops up onto the sink, her feet swinging back and forth. Her thin eyebrow arches, and I think of Abuelita's expression when I forget to do the dishes or leave the chicken out to thaw. "Oh, no. That's a bigger problem you'll have to deal with. And of course, you don't know who I am. They never talk about the ones they left behind." Her eyes dart across my face. "I'm Andaluz," she says, waiting for me to recognize her.

I suck in a breath. "But you're . . ."

"Dead?" Andaluz twists toward the mirror above the sink, taking in her gray skin and stringy black hair dripping with water. "Obviously." She looks me up and down again and smirks.

I pull myself up from the floor and wrap my arms around my waist, shivering from my wet clothes.

"Like I said, you've really done it now. But at least you have the gift. That should help." Andaluz stares at my arm and hops down from the sink. "Not that it ever helped me."

I edge closer to my violin case next to my backpack, not wanting Andaluz to get near my instrument. Even though it completely sabotaged me today, it's still my prized possession.

"What are you talking about?" I ask, my throat scratching. I yank up the sleeve of my hoodie, revealing the black stain on my skin. "Are you the one who's behind this?"

Andaluz's gaze darts from my arm to her reflection in the bathroom mirror. Her mouth sags and her shoulders droop. Reaching up to her wet hair, she winds a thin finger around a black strand, a snake coiling around her bony knuckle.

"Oh, that's not me. That's one hundred percent him." She shrugs. "You know, I thought the gift ended when our family came here. That we abandoned our magic in Cuba."

"What gift? What magic?" I say, inching closer to my violin. "You're not making any sense. I don't know who the *he* you keep talking about is! Is *he* why my day went so badly? Is *he* why I keep hearing water everywhere?"

Unwinding her finger from her hair, Andaluz waves her hand dismissively as her lip curls in a snarl. "Of course not. The water was obviously me. But the rest . . ." She shrugs. "It's all your fault, you know."

"What are you talking about?!" I ask.

"If I were you, I would be more respectful to the person who's explaining exactly what you've done to yourself, especially when she's here against her will." Andaluz takes a step toward me and leans over, bringing her face inches from mine. I'm overcome by the smell of seawater, an acidic saltiness making my eyes water. "You are cursed," she says.

She raises a finger and points to my violin, but I take a quick step forward and snatch the case off the sink, knocking my backpack to the floor in the process. My diary tumbles out and lands on the wet floor. Water slowly seeps into the pages. The puddles on the floor turn to black ink.

"Oh, you're going to come to regret that," Andaluz says as she watches the ink crawl up her legs, wrapping around her pale skin and seeping into her dress.

I take a step back and pick up the diary. The page where I recorded what Papi said about Andaluz is completely wet, the writing vanished from the soaked paper.

"Remember this, Mari: be careful who you call on from our family tree. We're not all fresh fruit." Andaluz staggers toward me as the black water travels up her torso and curls around her neck. "Some of us are rotten."

I stumble back and slip on the floor again. She's completely covered in murky liquid, and her body fades, the bathroom stall visible behind her as she slowly disappears.

Before I can say anything, she's gone. I'm left alone in the wet bathroom. The faucet still drips, sounding less like a ticking clock and more like a time bomb.

SIX

NO MATTER HOW many times I pick at the ropa vieja on my plate with my fork, no matter how many times I squeeze my eyes shut and shake my head, I can't erase the image of Andaluz, Abuelita's dead cousin, standing in a puddle and smirking. I can still hear her voice as she told me all this was my fault. My stomach churns as I wonder if I can believe anything Andaluz said, her snarling lips and black eyes making me question whether she was just trying to scare me.

But as horrifying as Andaluz was, who was she fighting with those columns of water? And why do I feel like *he's* so much worse?

"No need to kill that beef anymore," Liset says next to me, jutting out her chin at my plate. "It's already dead."

Abuelito chuckles and drums his fingers on the table, humming a song to himself.

I usually like the songs Abuelito sings, but his slow song

sounds off-key, the notes creeping under my skin and giving me chills. I remember the water sinking into my clothes in the bathroom, and I toss my fork onto the table with a clatter.

Mami and Papi stop their debate about whether the ropa vieja has enough garlic and look at me.

Abuelita jumps, her gray curls bouncing. "Pero mi cielo, ¿qué pasa?"

I sigh. "Nothing, Abuelita. Just the worst day ever." I mumble under my breath and take off my glasses, cleaning the scratched lens Mami hasn't noticed yet with my napkin and cramming them back on my face. I swear if I rub these glasses any more than I have today, with all the unbelievable things I've seen, they'll be paper-thin by morning.

Even if I manage to get the picture of Andaluz out of my mind amid the tornado of noise around me at the dinner table, it's quickly replaced with the image of my violin peg turning, whipping the string at my face. And I can still hear the drips. A knot settles in my throat, and I'm afraid I might throw up what little ropa vieja I've managed to swallow.

The mark on my arm tingles again, and I roll my wrist, trying to get rid of the feeling.

"I'm sure it wasn't that bad," Mami says, nudging my fork back to me.

I crumple my napkin in my hand. "Oh yeah? Mariachi

practice was the absolute worst, and I'm most definitely never going into any of the school bathrooms ever again. Like, never ever. Oh, and Ms. Faruqi assigned the stupidest project, when I really need to focus on my violin."

Liset chuckles. "Is she still making everybody do that world fair thing?"

I nod, smoothing out my napkin on my lap and then wadding it up again between my fingers. My knuckles turn white, and I remember Andaluz's grip on the bathroom stall as she crept toward me. My throat tightens, and I struggle to take a breath.

Stuffing a forkful of ropa vieja into her mouth, Liset shakes her head. "Yeah, she made my class do the same thing."

"Oh, that's an excellent project," Mami says. "There are so many interesting countries to learn about."

I feel my eyes rolling hard enough to start a car engine, but luckily Mami doesn't see me.

"Sí, pero no te olvides de que Cuba es el mejor de todos," Abuelito declares, lightly slapping his hand on the table.

"Papa, don't be silly," Papi says, nudging Abuelito with his elbow. He shakes his head and laughs. "Of course, you think Cuba is the best of them all."

No surprise. This is Peak Cubanity.

"Did you end up showcasing Cuba?" I ask Liset, eager to talk about anything that will get my mind off Andaluz.

"Ms. Faruqi wanted me to, but it wasn't like she was

making the other students present about Germany or England or Mexico. I love where our family is from, but why do I have to be an ambassador?"

I bite my lip and nod. Liset is right. We speak Spanish at home, eat Cuban food, and listen to Cuban music. My abuelitos are ambassadors enough for the whole family. Why do I have to be the one expert on all things Cuban for everyone in my class? I've never even been there.

"But you're missing a chance to tell everyone about where your family is from," Papi says.

Abuelito and Abuelita nod enthusiastically as Mami smiles. I'm definitely outnumbered. They do enough, telling everyone in town where we're from. I don't need to do an entire school presentation on it.

"So what country did you do?" I ask Liset.

Liset smiles. "Liechtenstein."

Abuelita raises her eyebrows. "¿Lique-qué? Eso no es un país."

Liset nods. "Yes, it is a country. It's in Europe."

Liset pulls out her cell phone from her jeans pocket and lays it on her thigh, out of Mami's sight and her "no phones at dinner" rule. She types on the screen, and her search pulls up a map of a tiny country between Germany, Switzerland, and Austria.

"Hey, phone away at the table," Mami says, poking her fork at me and Liset.

Liset slides her phone into her pocket. "Did you know that Liechtenstein once went to war with eighty soldiers and came back with eighty-one? I dressed up as the eighty-first soldier for the world fair."

"No way," I say.

Liset pulls out her phone again and types quickly, showing me an article about the Austro-Prussian War of 1866, where a soldier from the opposite side joined the Liechtenstein army.

Mami shakes her head, setting her fork on her plate. "It's like I'm invisible sometimes, right? Am I invisible?"

Papi laughs. "It's anarchy, mi amor."

While Liset, Mami, and Papi argue about the failed dinnertime cell phone policy, I hear Abuelito's voice, barely a whisper, rise above the noise.

"Tu tío fue soldado," he says, his lips pursed as he grips the edge of the dining room table.

Abuelita inhales sharply. "Ay, Nano," she says as everyone around the table quiets.

"Who was a soldier?" I ask.

Papi clears his throat. "Abuelito's talking about your great-uncle. He fought in the Bay of Pigs."

Abuelito nodded. "Baldomero Feijoo, mi hermano."

I didn't even know Abuelito had a brother. I shudder as I hear Andaluz's voice in my head.

They never talk about the ones they left behind.

"So what happened to him?" I ask.

Abuelito opens his mouth to answer but closes it again as he stares at his dinner plate.

Papi slides his hand over Abuelito's. "Everybody called him Pipo. He was one of the soldiers who tried to overthrow Castro in 1961. But they were captured by the Cuban army because they didn't have the support they were promised from the US government."

I look at Papi. I know that my abuelitos fled Cuba when Fidel Castro took power, because he took all the people's freedoms away. But I didn't know Abuelito had a brother.

Papi takes a deep breath and squeezes Abuelito's hand. "Pipo was executed in prison."

A silence falls over the table. Abuelito rises slowly and shuffles down the hallway, his shoulders sagging.

Papi turns toward me. "It's okay, kiddo. Sometimes the past is a heavy load to carry."

Now I get why Abuelito doesn't talk about his brother. Liset might be a complete metiche, bossing me around and always getting in my business, but I know if something happened to her, the hurt in my heart would choke me until I couldn't talk about it.

Mami gives me a soft smile, pushing around the rice on her plate with her fork. "So what country do you think you'll do for your project?"

I shrug. "I'm not sure. I haven't really decided."

Wanting to distract myself from the thought of having to do a school project, I shove a forkful of ropa vieja into my mouth.

And then it hits me.

My cheeks tingle, and my eyes water as an acidic flavor fills my mouth, burning my tongue. I swallow hard and cough, bits of shredded beef sticking to the corners of my mouth.

"Gross," Liset says. "Nice manners."

Mami gasps, and Papi covers his own grin with his napkin.

I reach for a strawberry candy from the bowl Abuelita always keeps on the table and stuff it into my mouth, hoping to erase the horrible taste of spoiled ropa vieja.

But my mouth drops open as the flavor of moldy cheese and sour, chunky milk pushes against the back of my throat. I gag and spit the candy out so hard, it flies across the table, landing on Abuelita's plate.

Abuelita throws her hands up in the air and shrieks as Liset doubles over, cackling.

"Nice job, Super Spitter," Liset says, smirking at me.

"It's not my fault Abuelita bought bad candies," I shoot back.

Abuelita slaps the table. "No son malas."

Liset grabs a candy from the bowl, unwraps it, and pops it into her mouth. I wait for her eyes to water and her face to turn red.

But nothing happens as Liset sucks on the candy, smiling. "Loquita," she says. "These are fine."

Once the sour taste in my mouth fades, I notice that the muscles on my forearm are tight, like someone is squeezing my arm with their hand. I want to check the mark on my skin, but I don't dare do it under Mami's and Abuelita's watchful eyes. Instead, I take deep breaths, waiting for the cramp to pass.

After dinner, as punishment for shooting rotten candy across the table, Mami makes me wash and dry all the dishes and put them away.

Even though we have a perfectly good dishwasher.

As I put the last plate away in the kitchen cabinet, I hear Papi dump a tin of dominoes out on the dining room table. The clattering sound calls Abuelito from his room, and he meanders down the hallway, taking a seat.

"I'm sorry I asked about your brother," I whisper to Abuelito as I sit down next to him.

Abuelito pats my hand. "No pasa nada, mi vida."

Even though Abuelito assures me it's okay, I can't help notice that his shoulders are still weighed down by people long gone. Maybe burning the effigies on New Year's Eve, like Abuelita always likes to do, really does clear a person of all their bad luck and sadness.

Or maybe some tears stick to your skin and never dry up.

Abuelito spreads a mountain of dominoes between us. Usually while we play, I tell Abuelito and Papi all about my day at school and the latest escapade of kindergartners trying to dig their way out of the school playground, prison-break style. But tonight, I tap a domino tile absent-mindedly on the table.

Abuelito chews on the stub of an unlit cigar, humming a soft, sad song as Papi sorts through the dominoes with his long fingers. When Abuelito gets to the chorus, he takes his cigar out of his mouth and begins to sing, his deep baritone voice swirling around the room. I drum the melody on my thigh with my fingers, as if I'm accompanying him on my violin.

"So exactly how bad was your mariachi practice?" Papi asks as we begin laying tiles down on the table, matching the dots on each other's dominoes.

"I don't want to talk about it," I say, pulling another domino from the pile. I try to focus on the splatter of dots on my tiles, but my lip quivers. I keep hearing the sound of my violin string snapping. My eyes prick with tears.

"Ay, mi vida, lo siento." Abuelito slides his hand across the table and covers my hand with his rough fingers.

My eyes sting. "Thanks. I really want to be in mariachi. And I know you don't get why—"

"Pero sí entiendo. La música es tu corazón, tu alma." Abuelito puts a hand over his heart as a hot tear slides down my cheek.

"Well, music may be my heart and soul, but if things keep going the way they are, I won't make the band. I'll be lucky if I graduate sixth grade!"

My tears fall freely now, and Papi brushes aside our carefully laid out game of dominoes as Abuelito takes both of my hands in his.

"Ay, mi vida, hay que echar fuera la mala suerte," Abuelito says.

I scratch under the sleeve of my hoodie at the thing that started it all—the mark on my arm. Ever since I held the effigy I was too embarrassed to burn, afraid that Mykenzye would see me, everything has gone wrong.

I rub my temples as the swirl of thoughts bangs against my eardrums and the back of my neck. Abuelito says I need to get rid of my bad luck. And the way our family does that is currently sitting squashed in the bottom of my backpack, a black splotch growing across its belly, so maybe the effigy is the key. Each horrible event, from my mariachi audition and disgusting dinner to everything in between, stands lined up like a domino pile, wobbling back and forth, ready to tumble. I wince as I scrape too hard against my skin and wonder if the first tile will fall before I can fix this, knocking down all the others and burying me under the weight of bad luck.

SEVEN

I WAKE UP the next morning, my blue sheets twisted in knots around my legs and my pillows thrown on the floor. My whole body aches as I get out of bed, worn out from a restless night of fitful sleep.

I yank the doll out of my backpack, forgetting in my exhaustion that I'd told myself not to touch it again, and stare at it with narrow eyes. I examine every stitch and inch of fabric. The black spot on the belly has grown, fully covering the chest now. The pink floral fabric from Papi's favorite vacation shirt doesn't look so innocent anymore.

I tuck the doll under the pillow on my bed, promising myself to deal with it after school.

At breakfast, Abuelita raises her eyebrows at me when I almost fall asleep in my bowl of Cinnamon Toast Crunch. Abuelito takes one look at the scowl plastered on my face and declares that I've woken up with el moño virado.

Peak Cubanity that I'm too tired to document in my diary.

Besides, I know I didn't wake up just in a bad mood. I've woken up with something else—an uneasy feeling that seems to grow like the black spot on the effigy hiding under my pillow. It started off small in my stomach but has expanded to my chest, pushing on my ribs and stinging when I take a deep breath.

Not even Abuelita's Vivaporu could fix it.

The school bus brakes screech outside, and I hop up from my chair, grabbing my backpack.

"Allí viene la guagua," Abuelita says, declaring that the bus has arrived.

"Oye, loquita. Forgetting something? Again?" Liset asks, her permanent eye roll punctuating her questions.

I shake my head. "Don't have practice today," I explain, secretly glad I have a small break from the chaos of my mariachi practice yesterday. Maybe by tomorrow I'll have figured out how to keep violin strings from taking on a life of their own.

Rushing out the door, I give Abuelito a kiss on the cheek just in time to see the school bus rumble away from my house. I sigh and shake my head, hurrying up the sidewalk. Hopefully today won't be an epic disaster like yesterday.

I pass a house with plywood on the windows and a tarp over the roof. A hurricane came through two years ago, and there are still houses like that all over Port Ballí. Papi says everybody recovers at a different rate when bad things happen.

I spot Keisha ahead of me on the sidewalk, her face buried in her phone.

"Did you miss the bus too?" I ask, catching up to her, the sweat growing on the back of my neck from my thick hoodie that covers the mark on my arm. The sun seems to hang closer to the ground in Port Ballí, even in January. I wait for my phone to buzz, thinking she was sending a message to the Super Ojos group chat. But it doesn't, and I realize she was probably texting Syed. Again.

Keisha nods. "It didn't even stop at the corner! Just drove right by!" She rolls her shoulders and stuffs her phone into her back pocket. "Syed said he always gets to his bus stop fifteen minutes early."

I roll my eyes. I'm used to the Super Ojos being me, Keisha, and Juan Carlos. This shift in our group feels like when Mami tries to add potatoes to picadillo. It just doesn't work.

"What?" Keisha asks, catching my expression.

"Nothing." I shrug as laughing gulls circle overhead, hoping we'll drop any breakfast crumbs we might have.

"Whatever. But listen." She lifts the sleeve of her shirt and shows me a long black stain running up the top of her forearm. When the skin on my arm starts to burn, I scratch at the spot. Keisha's eyes dart to my hand, and I stop.

"This for serious isn't a fencing bruise," she says.

"Oh. Hopefully it'll go away soon," I tell Keisha. I've never wished for anything more in my life. Whatever this mark is and whatever it's doing to me, I don't want Keisha to have to go through the same thing.

Keisha groans. "And fencing practice was super weird yesterday. Nothing seemed to go right."

Andaluz's high-pitched voice creeps up my back and sits on my shoulder, slithering in my ear and telling me I'm cursed. And now, so is Keisha.

My skin crawls, and I shudder, remembering Andaluz's dripping figure in the bathroom. As much as I don't want to accept it, I don't think she could have been lying.

While we stand across the street from school, waiting for passing cars, I decide to tell Keisha the truth about the marks on our arms and the curse, but a sharp rip stops me. I feel the weight of my backpack drop off my shoulders.

"Oh, no!" Keisha gasps as we watch my backpack sink into a muddy puddle next to the sidewalk, soaking up all the brown water.

Grabbing the backpack as fast as I can, I mutter, "What the frijoles? How is there even a puddle here? We haven't had rain in a week."

I inspect the folders and books. They're all completely

soaked, the ink swirling on my papers like a kindergartner's finger painting. I shake my head.

"You can borrow from me today," Keisha offers.

"Assuming I don't get struck by lightning first."

"Or attacked by a pack of rabid squirrels," Kiesha says, a smile creeping across her lips.

I hold my dripping backpack away from my body as Keisha and I cross the street. I hear the click-clack of Juan Carlos's skateboard wheels as he heads toward us.

"I hope he's had a better morning than we've had," I say.

"Maybe he found a finger in his oatmeal," Keisha shoots back.

I think for a moment. "Or all his underwear turned to sandpaper."

"Super Ojos!" Juan Carlos shouts. He waves at us, pushing his left foot off the ground twice and speeding across the street.

I look around and think of all the things that could go wrong in this moment. He could get sucked into a pothole in the street. A distracted driver on their cell phone could absolutely clobber him. A flock of pelicans sailing overhead could use him as a bathroom.

But nothing happens. Juan Carlos glides toward us and hops off his skateboard.

Because he never touched the effigy. He doesn't have a mark.

Looking down at the grass next to the sidewalk, I spot five black lizards squirming toward me. Their scales glisten green and purple in the morning sunlight. They aren't like any lizard I've ever seen in Texas. I take a step toward Keisha and watch as all five of them follow my shoes with their heads, their tongues darting in and out of their mouths. I immediately think of the lizards squirming out of the faucet in the bathroom.

I've got a lot to explain to Keisha, but as the lizards inch toward me one spiny toe at a time, I tell myself it can wait. There are too many other strange things happening.

"You ready to go?" Juan Carlos asks.

"Yes. Definitely," I say.

Once school starts, I cross my fingers, toes, and nose hairs, hoping the day doesn't get any worse. At least I'm not hearing drips of water anymore. That's something.

"Juan Carlos, if you keep tapping that pen, I'm going to run you through with it," Keisha says with narrowed eyes in the middle of Ms. Faruqi's social studies class as we push our desks together. My backpack sits shoved under my desk in a trash bag Mr. Nguyen gave me during first period. Mykenzye asked if my mom had given it to me. I was confused at first and then realized that Mykenzye thought Ms. Rosales, the school custodian, was my mom. I wonder if she thinks Juan Carlos is my brother.

Juan Carlos grips his pen and mutters, "Sorry. Just trying to figure out what country to do for my project."

"You're not going to talk about El Salvador?" I ask. "I bet your mom could help you with it."

Juan Carlos chuckles. "Yeah. She'd be all over that. But it might be kind of cool to learn about somewhere new."

I smile as Juan Carlos starts scribbling jellyfish on his paper.

"Well, I'm picking Costa Rica," Keisha says excitedly. "My moms and I went there two years ago, and it was amazing. We got to go zip-lining through the rain forest and see sloths." She pauses from filling up a third page with notes and ideas about Costa Rica and then asks, "What about you, Mari?"

I shrug and bite my lip. "I don't know. I think my abuelos would probably want me to tell everybody about Cuba, but I don't know how much help they would be. I mean, we speak Spanish at home, eat Cuban food, and my abuelito listens to Cuban music pretty much nonstop, but that's it. I don't know anything else."

Except my abuelita's newly discovered cousin and Abuelito's brother—both of which I had no idea ever existed until the last couple of days.

"But that's the important stuff, right?" Juan Carlos offers, adding a sea turtle drawing next to the jellyfish on his paper.

"What do you mean?" I ask.

"Well, you could look up Cuba's population or type of government or historical events and then bore everybody to death with your presentation." Juan Carlos squints at the tip of his pen and shakes it before continuing his doodling. "It's better if you actually know the real stuff about a country, like the people, right?"

"Exactly," Keisha says, nodding. "I don't think I would've picked Costa Rica if I hadn't actually been there and gotten to experience everything. Did you know they were the first country in Latin America to legalize same-sex marriage?"

I clear my throat and nod. "But it's not like I can go to Cuba."

I've sat through a mountain of dinners where my parents and abuelitos argued about the US travel restrictions or the embargo against Cuba. I wasn't sure what an embargo was, but I figured out it meant the United States wouldn't trade with Cuba.

Juan Carlos shrugs. "Yeah, but that's where your abuelos can help you out. And once Keisha finishes her brilliant presentation in about five minutes, she can help you too," he says, winking.

Keisha laughs. "Yeah, it's gonna take more than five minutes. I'm a little slower than usual today. My awful fencing practice is still clogging my brain."

"What happened?" I ask, my upper lip starting to sweat

as I dread Keisha's answer. Images of my mariachi practice float back, and the mark on my arm tingles again.

"Well, any more of these practices, and I'll never make the Houston team. It all started out fine. Coach put me with the high school fencers, which was cool. But then it was like my shoes were covered with superglue or something. I'd try to advance, but my feet were stuck in place. I basically had to stand there while my opponents stabbed me."

"Was there something wrong with the mats?" I ask, wondering if this was the same thing that made my feet stick to the kitchen floor yesterday morning. I notice Juan Carlos flip to a clean page in his notebook and start doodling while biting his lip.

"I don't think so. It was only happening to me. If it was the mats, everyone would've had problems. I'm the only one who lost all her bouts."

I tug on the sleeve of my hoodie. "I'm sorry. That sucks."

Keisha waves her arms in the air. "Oh, that's not even all of it! My fencing jacket tried to kill me. I could barely breathe with it on."

Juan Carlos looks up from his notebook. "How's that possible? Is it the right size?"

Blowing a black curl off her forehead, Keisha sighs. "Of course. But when I zipped it over my chest protector, it shrunk. Like three sizes. I could hardly take a breath. It didn't make any sense."

Juan Carlos goes back to scribbling in his notebook. My mind flashes to the peg on the neck of my violin, tightening until the string snapped and flew at my cheek. I thought there wasn't any explanation for that either until Andaluz told me I was cursed. My palms sweat, and I wipe them on my jeans.

I look at Keisha as she bites her nails and narrows her eyes. She's obsessed with fencing. When all the kids in third grade were joining soccer and Little League, Keisha's moms took her to Houston to watch a fencing tournament. Keisha marveled at the intimidating masks and blades of the white-uniformed competitors who were sparring with each other, and she was hooked. She immediately convinced her moms to let her learn.

As Keisha scratches the black mark under her sleeve, my stomach rolls, knowing this is all my fault. Because she touched my effigy, her fencing practices are a mess. I should've just thrown it in the fire on New Year's Eve. But I didn't, and now it's lying under my pillow, the creepy, moldy splotch growing on its belly.

I start to ask Juan Carlos to draw me a World's Worst Friend T-shirt, but I bite my lip instead.

"All right," Juan Carlos says to Keisha, snapping me from my thoughts. "I've designed a training system for you. Now maybe you can deal with your new . . . challenges."

He slides his notebook across our group of desks and

shows us his drawings. I see a fencing jacket with a large tag hanging under the armpit that says "Pull for puffer-fish mode." Next to it is a sketch of the shoes Keisha normally wears with her fencing uniform, but now blobs are sticking out from the bottom of the soles.

"And how will changing her uniform help?" I ask.

Juan Carlos flips his black hair off his forehead. "I figure if her jacket keeps shrinking, she'll need an emergency release that puffs it up so she can breathe. And if we put jellyfish on her shoes, that'll keep her from getting stuck to the mat."

Keisha smiles and pats Juan Carlos on the back. "Sounds good to me. I'll try anything."

"Maybe you can make something for me," I mumble.

"What happened to you?" Juan Carlos asks.

I tell him all about the malfunctioning music stand, the swirling music notes, and the possessed violin string. As his eyes grow wider, I decide it's best to leave out meeting Andaluz in the bathroom. Especially since I can hardly still believe it myself.

Keisha slams her notebook shut, startling me. "What the heck is causing all this?"

I swallow hard and twist my hands in my lap. Abuelito's words from last night come back to me. I know what I should've done to keep from getting cursed. And now I know what I have to do. "I think it's because on New Year's Eve, I didn't burn the effigy my abuela made."

Juan Carlos raises an eyebrow. "You mean that creepy doll that was sticking out of your backpack?"

Keisha narrows her eyes, thinking, as she chews on the end of her pencil. "Do you really think that's true? All that bad luck stuff?"

I sigh, pulling on the hem of my hoodie. The mark on my arm feels hot again, and I resist the urge to peek at it to see if it's spread like the splotch on the effigy. "I'm not entirely sure. But maybe?"

"That can't be possible," Keisha says. "I mean, not to offend your family tradition, but it just seemed like something fun y'all do together. Not something that actually accomplishes anything." She taps the tip of her pencil hard enough on her paper to form a hole.

I take a deep breath and slide the sleeve of my hoodie up to my elbow, revealing the inky black mark sitting on my forearm.

Keisha gasps, holding her arm next to mine, the splotches on our skin looking like a pair of crocodiles slithering up from our wrists.

"You have it too!" Keisha says. "What is it?"

I really don't want Keisha to be mad at me, but I have to tell her the truth.

"It's because you touched the effigy that was in my backpack. It's making us have bad luck." My stomach flip-flops. "It's cursed us."

Keisha's mouth settles in a hard line. I wait for her to say something; I want the chance to reassure her that I have a plan to fix everything, but she pulls her phone out of her pocket. I lean over and see that she's texting Syed.

A groan erupts from my throat before I can stop it, and Keisha's gaze flashes to me.

"What?" she snaps.

"Nothing." I cross my arms and press my lips together. "This is just kind of a big deal. Don't you think you can stop texting Syed long enough so we can figure out this curse together?"

"Excuse me?" Keisha says.

When I don't say anything else, Keisha gives me a hard look. I can't believe she's more upset by what I said about Syed than about the actual curse. She quickly gathers her things and gets up from her desk, stomping over to an open seat next to Ceci Baumgartner.

Juan Carlos gives me a sympathetic smile and shrugs as I try to go back to my classwork. I don't know why Keisha isn't focused on what's important right now. It's definitely not Syed. He's not part of this problem.

The wind outside picks up, and I watch the leaves from the oak trees swirl on the ground. A few plaster themselves to the classroom window, sliding along the glass. Other leaves join them in the increasing breeze until they form a pattern. I squint at the window and gasp.

GOOD . . . LUCK

Before I can elbow Juan Carlos to show him, the wind brushes the leaves off the glass and they're gone. Heat rises to my cheeks as I remember the same message written in the bathroom mirror. I'm being taunted.

I shake my head, trying to forget all the strange events that are stalking me. I reach into the trash bag holding all my wet school supplies to find a piece of paper dry enough to use. I need to distract myself from the frown Keisha keeps throwing in my direction.

My hand wraps around the diary Abuelita gave me, and I pull it out. The pages that got wet in the bathroom yesterday are dry now, so I flip to a new page and tap my pencil on my desk.

Maybe Juan Carlos is right. Maybe if I decide to present Cuba for the world showcase, I should talk about people. Abuelita would want me to write about our family anyway.

I brush my hand across the page of the diary and write at the top,

Baldomero Feijoo

Continuing on the paper, I write,

My abuelito's brother, Baldomero Feijoo, was a soldier. He fought in the Bay of Pigs. He was captured and killed in prison.

He was older than my abuelito. That's all I know about him because I didn't even know that Abuelito had a brother.

I read over my sentences. It's not much, but maybe Abuelito can give me more information if he feels like talking about it.

After I close the diary, I glance at Keisha and catch her staring at the mark on my arm. She looks away and back to her phone. I tug my sleeve down and lay my head on my desk.

As my arm aches, I hear soft music swirling down the hallways of school, meandering into the classroom, around my desk, and up the back of my neck.

EIGHT

AFTER SCHOOL, I trudge up the steps to my house, the beginnings of a headache creeping across my scalp and sinking into my tangled hair. I don't know how long I can take school days like the one I just had. Thick pill bugs squirmed out of my chicken sandwich at lunch, every pencil I used turned into a biting stick bug, and I choked on a cloud of mosquitoes that seemed to attack only me during P.E.

Abuelito's seat on the porch is empty. He plays dominoes in the town park most afternoons, but as I pass his chair, I notice three fat spiders with hairy legs crawling up the back. I run through the door and plop down on the couch in the living room, glad that Liset won't be home from school for a while. The house is quiet, with Mami and Papi still teaching and Abuelita out buying groceries, sewing supplies, or bathtub-size jars of Vivaporu.

I head to my bedroom and reach under the pillow on

my bed, grabbing the effigy Abuelita sewed. I trace my fingers along the threads that hold the seams together. They're stretched tight across the fabric, as if the doll has been inflated with more stuffing than before, but I know that's not possible. The black splotch on the chest is still the same size, the moldy hue covering the flowers like a disease.

I pull out my phone and drop a message into the Super Ojos group chat.

I think I know how to fix everything and get rid of the bad luck. I'm going to burn the effigy like I should've all along.

Juan Carlos texts back a GIF of out-of-control fireworks setting a backyard on fire.

Keisha doesn't respond. I hope she hasn't blocked me. I hope I can get rid of the curse before she's completely fed up with me.

Maybe burning the effigy will make all this bad luck stop for me and Keisha. I don't even care if Mykenzye is already home and staring out the window. It'll be worth it.

Walking to the kitchen, I grab a box of matches from a drawer. The effigy squirms in my hand as I go out to the backyard and stand over the firepit.

I hold the doll in front of me and say, "Okay, Abuelitos. I guess your Peak Cubanity is true. So here's all the bad luck. There's got to be a ton."

I scan around the yard and look over to Mocosa Mykenzye's house. Her window is empty. I'm all alone.

Except for the mango tree in the corner of the grass. A thick black snake is wrapped around its trunk, slithering farther up the tree in a tight coil. I push my glasses along the bridge of my nose and squint. The snake doesn't look like any I've ever seen before in Texas.

But I've got bigger problems than an escaped animal from Port Ballí Wildlife Center.

Setting the doll in the pit, I draw a match and light it. The head of the match burns bright, but as I hold it close to the firepit, an unusually warm breeze kicks up and blows out the flame.

Groaning, I toss the useless match into the firepit, pull another match from the box, and light it. Kneeling closer to the effigy, I throw the match directly on top of it and watch as the flame dances, slightly licking the fabric of the doll.

Soon this will all be over. The flames will eat up the doll, getting rid of my bad luck along with Keisha's. If I can manage to do all this without my family finding out that I set a fire by myself when they weren't home, I'll be free.

But the flame goes out. It disappears from the effigy without even blackening the fabric.

"Oh, come on," I mutter under my breath.

Before I can light another match, I hear a violin playing. Slow and soft at first, but then speeding up. I look up at Mocosa Mykenzye's window, but it's closed.

The music swirls around me in the breeze, and I glance

at the black snake on the mango tree. It stops slithering up the trunk and coils tighter around the bark, flicking its tongue in and out. Hot pressure rises on the mark under my sleeve.

I light another match, and then another and another, each time their flames blowing out in the breeze that seems to rustle only the avocado trees in our backyard but not the persimmon trees in Mykenzye's yard.

"You've got to be kidding me," I say, stomping my foot on the ground.

I yank the effigy from the firepit and hold it under my arm. Lighting the final match from the box, I shove the flame directly under the foot of the doll.

A hot breeze tickles the back of my neck and makes my skin crawl as a shiver dances down my spine. The flame on the match head extinguishes in a trail of light gray smoke that curls up into the air.

A voice sits on my shoulder, a low growl whispering in my ear, *Not yet.*

My head whips around the yard, searching for the source of the voice as my heart beats in my ears. The mark on my skin burns, as if I'd held my last match to it, and I drop the effigy. Cradling my arm to my chest, I breathe hard.

A growl fills the yard, and I fall to the ground as I see a man walk out from behind a mango tree. His eyes are narrowed and dark, his fists clenched at his sides.

"Get out of here," he hisses, staring at something over my shoulder.

The music speeds up, a violin playing at a frantic pace. It's so loud, I wince and cover my ears.

The man storms toward me, and I stumble back onto the grass, my fingers digging into the dirt. I think of the person whose shadow flashed on the bathroom wall as Andaluz fought him, and my breath catches in my throat.

"I'm sorry. I'm sorry," I mumble. "I didn't mean to do anything."

He stops in front of me and crouches down. His eyes scan my face. I hold my breath.

"Are you all right?" he asks.

"Wh . . . what?" I stammer. I realize that his voice sounds different from the first one I heard. It's softer.

"Did he hurt you? Are you all right?"

I shake my arm as the burning feeling disappears. "I think I'm okay. Maybe."

Looking at the man's face, I see the same long, thin nose that Abuelito has. Golden brown eyes just like Papi's stare at me. He flips dark hair off his forehead, straighter than mine but the same color.

"Who are you?" I ask.

The man smiles, and my heartbeat fades from pounding in my ears.

"Baldomero Feijoo. My brother called me Pipo."

I blink, taking a moment to believe what he just said. And then I remember. Inching away from him, I ask, "So you're a ghost too?"

The smile on Pipo's face grows. "Too? Oh, that's right. You met Andaluz."

I nod, pulling my knees to my chest and wrapping my arms around my legs. I stare at the bright yellow paint on Mykenzye's house, more faded on the south side from being beaten by sun and sand. I can't bring myself to make eye contact with Pipo.

Pipo sits down next to me on the grass and crosses his legs. I glance at the worn khaki-colored button-down shirt and dark brown pants he's wearing. He shakes his head. "Don't worry. I'm not like her. She's . . . hurt. But she won't show up unless you call on her again."

"But I didn't call on her. She just appeared in the school bathroom. Crawled right out of a stall sopping wet, like from a horror movie. And not one of the good ones."

Pipo raises an eyebrow. "Are you sure?"

I roll my eyes. "Yeah. I'm pretty sure I didn't summon some dead cousin to make me pee my pants."

I look at Pipo and bite my lip, the realization of who I'm talking to hitting me. My stomach rumbles, and I wrap my arms tighter around my knees. I lean forward, breathing deep.

"You have a gift, Mari. Just like Andaluz and just like me."

I take another deep breath. "That's what Andaluz said. What the frijoles are you talking about?"

Pipo chuckles. "Well, think about it. Did you do something before Andaluz showed up in the bathroom? Something that you also did before I showed up?"

I think for a moment. "I wrote about both of you in the diary Abuelita gave me for New Year's. Is that it?"

Pipo smiles. "What did you write about me?"

I loosen the grip on my legs and relax a little. "You . . . you were my abuelito's brother. You fought in the Bay of Pigs, but you were captured. And Castro's soldiers killed you in prison."

Pipo bites his lip. "Is that all they told you about me?" he asks, his voice floating in the yard. A flock of pelicans fly overhead, sailing on the gulf breeze.

I nod. I don't know how to tell him that up until yesterday, I didn't even know he existed.

"I wasn't just a soldier, you know. I played the violin, like you. I had a dog named Caramelo. I was going to ask Eugenia Vargas to marry me. You should write that down too."

Taking a deep breath, I run my fingers through my ponytail. "So let's say I did write that other stuff about you in the diary. What would that mean? You'd keep showing up?"

Pipo points a finger at me and clicks his tongue. "That's

it. The Feijoos on your Abuelito's side and the Crespos on your Abuelita's side have been able to call on the dead for generations. It was a fantastic stroke of luck, maybe even fate, that brought two magical families together when your abuelitos married. We've all been able to summon our ancestors in different ways. You can apparently do it by writing things down. I did it playing the violin."

I bite my lip and grunt. "That's not fair. I should be able to do it with my violin too. My handwriting is the worst."

Pipo laughs, and his voice carries through the backyard. "Your abuelito didn't always like my playing. He used to stomp through our house covering his ears and sticking his tongue out at me."

I try to picture my abuelito as a little boy younger than me, and I can't do it. We don't have any pictures of him from when he was in Cuba. "Well, music is like his favorite thing ever now. Right behind Abuelita's arroz con leche."

Pipo smiles. "But you're the first in the family to have the gift since we left the island. That makes you pretty special."

I groan. "We're gonna have to disagree on that."

The mark on my arm itches, and I scratch it without thinking. Pipo watches me with narrowed eyes.

I slowly raise the sleeve of my Houston Aeros hoodie and hold out my arm to him. "So does this have anything to do with my special power?"

Pipo shakes his head, and his gaze grows serious. "I'm afraid that's something else entirely. Something we'll have to figure out."

I pull on the hem of my hoodie. "Is this curse—and all the bad luck Keisha and I have—really because I didn't burn the effigy Abuelita made?"

Pipo pulls a long blade of grass from the lawn and holds it between his fingers. "I think it might be. We burned effigies in Cuba, too. Your abuelito would always draw a monster face on his. Every year. Our parents told us the effigies absorb all the bad luck and sadness we'd had over the past year. When we burn them on New Year's Eve, a luck eater consumes them. That's how he gets his food."

I think about what Pipo is saying. Burning effigies isn't just a Peak Cubanity tradition. It's something that reminds my abuelitos of home.

"But what's a luck eater?" I ask.

Flicking the blade of grass in the air, Pipo shrugs. "They're the ones that eat up all the bad luck. When you didn't burn your effigy, you starved him. Or her, I guess. Maybe this one wants to make you as miserable as possible for it."

I put my head in my hands. The headache that was crawling across my scalp has sunk in and squeezed my brain. I don't know if I want to laugh, scream, or cry. I might do all three.

"I think it's a him," I mutter. "That's how Andaluz talked about the Luck Eater when she fought him off. And the voice I heard before you showed up didn't sound like yours. It sounded like a him, too. A horrible, terrible him."

"We'll figure it out, Mari. Trust me," Pipo says.

But when I look up, he's fading away. Before I can say anything, he disappears, vanishing from the backyard as the sea breeze picks up.

I'm left staring at the snake, still wrapped around the mango tree, its blackened gaze never leaving the effigy cradled in my arms.

NINE

SITTING AT THE kitchen table that evening with my diary tucked in the pocket of my hoodie, I can't bring myself to dive into Abuelita's empanadas de picadillo. Bad luck and ghost relatives have destroyed my appetite. I can still hear the voice from the backyard slithering up my neck and into my ear.

I try to control my breathing, but it gets shallower and faster as I think about my family. I wouldn't even be in this horrible situation if we didn't have the tradition of burning effigies. If we were just like every family, I would've had a normal mariachi practice, and no one would be popping up in the school bathroom or my backyard.

This is entirely the fault of Peak Cubanity.

I reach for one of the empanadas, but a pain in my ankle stops me. I brush my leg with my fingers and gasp. A thick black beetle crawls over my big toe. I yelp and kick my leg out, earning an eyebrow raise from Abuelita.

I blink, and the beetle disappears.

Before I can react, the glass of water next to my plate turns black. A squirming worm, just like the ones that I thought filled my pencil case, emerges from the water and drapes itself over the edge of the cup. I snap my gaze to Abuelito, sitting next to me, but he's busy tapping his fingers on the table and humming a song. When I look back at the glass, the water is clear and the worm is gone.

I clutch the diary tighter in my hand and shake my head.

I'm stuck. I need to burn the effigy to get rid of my bad luck, but this Luck Eater thing won't let me. So now I have to figure out how to get rid of the Luck Eater, make the bad luck go away, and fix things between Keisha and me.

And never mind the teeny-tiny piece of information I learned from Pipo about having some magical ability to summon my dead relatives. I can't even wrap my brain around that one completely without almost passing out.

This is going to be harder than getting Abuelito to listen to something other than Cuban music or Abuelita to make something other than Cuban food. I look at my plate, wanting to bite into the crispy pastries filled with spiced ground beef, olives, and raisins, but my appetite is buried under the waves rolling in my stomach.

The front door slams, pushing me from my thoughts.

Mami and Liset march into the dining room, and Liset

tosses her backpack in the corner. She immediately points at the empanadas. "Nothing makes me hungrier than powerlifting practice," she says. "That and outlifting Nathan Miller. He didn't know what hit him today."

Mami follows, sitting down next to Papi and laying her head on his shoulder. She's always worn out after her day at the high school, teaching English to speakers of other languages.

Abuelita passes her a plate with two empanadas, and everyone dives in. I pick at the pastry crust, still not able to bring myself to eat anything.

"So, Mari, have you decided what country you're going to do for the school fair?" Mami asks, wiping the corners of her mouth with her napkin.

I take a deep breath. Ms. Faruqi's project is the last thing on my mind, buried beneath all the bad luck and the sudden appearance of my tío abuelo, Pipo.

"Cuba, I guess." I shrug. It seems as good a choice as any.

A smile breaks out on Abuelito's face, and he slaps the table. "Así es."

"Good choice, kiddo," Papi says, winking at Abuelito. "Just don't interview your abuelito about it or he'll be telling you that Cuba invented coffee and salsa music. Qué paquete."

"Pero no es mentira." Abuelito raises his arms in surrender, denying the lie.

While everyone dives into Peak Cubanity and argues about whether Cubans are the best in the world at baseball, I lean over to Abuelito and tug on the sleeve of his shirt. "Abuelito? Can I ask you something?"

"Sí, mi vida," he answers.

I bite my lip, wondering how much I can ask him without seeming suspicious. But I think I need more info about Pipo so I can make him show up again, if what he said about my power is true.

I scoot closer to Abuelito. "I . . . I don't want to make you upset again. But I was wondering something."

Abuelito places his hand over mine and nods.

"Did your brother Pipo have a dog named Caramelo?"

A smile breaks out on Abuelito's face. "Ay, ese ratón. Un tornado de ruido que siempre robaba mi comida."

I laugh. "The dog stole your food?"

Abuelito chuckles, searching my face. "¿Pero cómo lo supiste?"

"Oh, um, I heard Abuelita mention it, I think," I reply, not wanting to tell Abuelito that I'd actually learned it from Pipo himself.

"Yo quería un gato, pero mi hermano quería un perro. Y como él era mayor, ganó." Abuelito winks at me and shrugs.

I groan. "That's so unfair. That happens with me and Liset all the time. Just because she's older, she gets what she wants. Sorry you didn't get to have a cat."

Abuelito chuckles and pats me on the leg.

My phone buzzes in my pocket, and I slide it from my jeans so Mami can't catch me with it out at the table. I see a text from Keisha.

It's getting worse. My fencing blade shot sparks out of the tip today at practice. Coach is about to kick me off the team. If you've already burned the effigy, it didn't work. We need to fix this.

Excusing myself quickly, I run to my room with my diary. Opening it to the page where I had written about Pipo, I quickly scribble all the information he told me in the backyard, adding what Abuelito told me too. I hope it's enough to make him appear.

Do I have to do anything else? Shout "Alabao" or sing Celia Cruz?

It wouldn't surprise me if Peak Cubanity was what made this thing work.

Typing a quick text back to Keisha, I tell her, I couldn't burn the effigy. Can we meet up? I can explain in person.

I'm not sure my friends will believe me when I tell them about the Luck Eater. They might laugh and call me a loquita like Liset does.

But I also don't want to risk Keisha's fencing dreams by bringing any more bad luck.

I clutch the diary to my chest again while I sit on my bed. Looking across the room, I spot the effigy on the floor in the corner. The floral fabric is almost completely covered in thick, fuzzy mold. My eyes widen as the head of the doll shakes. The fabric rips, and a dark green lizard squirms its way out of where an eye would be. It perches on top of the effigy and looks at me.

Gasping, I squeeze my eyes shut. When I open them again, the lizard is gone and the effigy is whole.

My breath quickens and my shoulders heave. Tears prick the corners of my eyes, and I bury my face in the diary.

I glance at the page, and the words I wrote about Pipo swirl before my eyes. They dance across the paper, twisting and bouncing until they resemble sheet music. A soft melody I've heard Abuelito hum a thousand times floats through the window.

I take a deep breath. Help is on the way.

TEN

I WAKE UP with a yelp on Saturday morning, running my hands quickly through my hair. I dreamed of spiny cockroaches and squirming worms making their home on my scalp, the bugs creeping down my neck and into the collar of my pajamas. I can still feel them, and I shiver as goose bumps rise on my arms.

I'm thankful it's Saturday and I don't have to plan for anything going wrong at school. Or for seeing anything that's not really there in the halls of Port Ballí Primary School. I don't want to even think about the possible minefield of ghost relatives popping up in bathrooms, sabotaged violins, and lizards pouring out of my backpack. Or Mocosa Mykenzye seeing me freak out when a phantom snake crawls up my nose.

But dealing with everything at home is just as dangerous.

With narrowed eyes I inspect the huevo con arroz y plátano that Abuelita made for breakfast, hoping the Luck

Eater won't glue my mouth shut with the mushy banana or turn the rice into maggots. I look inside my shoes to make sure there aren't any spiders waiting to nibble on my toes. I carefully run a comb through my hair, hoping it won't fall out in tangled clumps.

It's exhausting. The permanent stomachache I have from worrying makes Mami take my temperature. Abuelita tries to slather my hands with Vivaporu when I won't stop biting my nails. At the breakfast table, Abuelito asks me if I'm tapping out the rhythm of a new song with my nervously bouncing leg.

Where's Pipo when I need him? Did that diary thing really work or not?

As I walk to Zaragoza Park in the middle of Port Ballí to meet Keisha, my diary clutched in my arms, I make sure not to scuff my feet, in case the sidewalk decides to roll like the gulf waves and trip me. I give myself a headache shifting my gaze from the ground to the sky to check if any of the terns or kingfishers I love watching at the beach are going to dive-bomb me or use my hair as a toilet.

I take a deep breath and think of the game Mami taught me in third grade when I was upset about Connor McKinney making fun of the leftover pork tamales I'd brought for lunch. For each letter of the alphabet, Mami and I brainstormed a silly phrase to describe what was stressing me out. Mami told me she had come up with her own Insult

Dictionary when she had to deal with ignorant comments from people who didn't like her students.

I purse my lips and think as I walk along past the shops on the beach. I pass the Ballí T-Shirt Emporium, with its large plaster great white shark whose sharp-toothed mouth you have to walk through to get inside. Dulcita Paleta Shop has a sign declaring one free Popsicle for each bag of beach trash you turn in.

"This Luck Eater is an absolutely awful alpaca . . . a boiling bloody blister . . . a crusty cheese cough drop," I mutter to myself.

I'm in the middle of thinking up insults starting with the letter *D* when a man steps out from the alley next to Dulcita Paleta Shop and onto the sidewalk. He stands in my path before I can change course. I wince, expecting to collide with him, but instead I walk right through him and tumble forward.

Catching myself, I turn around and see the same brown pants and khaki shirt that appeared in my yard yesterday. "What the frijoles? Pipo, you scared me!"

He smiles. "I'm sorry! I'm still getting used to people being able to see me."

I scan Pipo's appearance. He's more solid now, and I can't see the palm trees lining the sidewalk behind him. But if I stare long enough, I notice that his shape is wavy, like the surface of water that's been broken by a thrown rock.

Every so often, a faint red splotch grows on the fabric of his khaki shirt and then fades away just as quickly. To someone not really paying attention, he looks like the guys who take fishing charters out on the gulf, not a Cuban exile from sixty years ago.

"It worked!" I tell him. "I wrote about you in the diary again, and you showed up!"

He smiles and winks at me. "It's a pretty great ability, isn't it?"

My mind flashes to Andaluz's wet form standing over me in the bathroom. "Sometimes."

Pipo shoves his hands into the pockets of his pants. "So did you talk about me yesterday?"

I nod. "Abuelito told me that Caramelo used to steal his food. He said your dog was a noise tornado and that he really wanted a cat."

Pipo raises his head and laughs, his voice filling the air. I smile as my heart warms at the sound, just like Abuelito's deep laugh.

Pipo puts his hands on his hips, his shoulders still bouncing with laughter. "You should ask him how he got the scar over his left eyebrow. I'll give you a hint. It involves a race up a coconut tree."

I look at Pipo, his dark brown hair swept across his forehead, his thin fingers tapping on his thigh. As we continue walking down the sidewalk toward Zaragoza Park,

I tell him, "The bad luck got worse last night, you know. Keisha had a horrible fencing practice. And I keep seeing things that aren't really there. At least I hope they're not."

My foot catches on a raised piece of pavement in the sidewalk, and I stumble forward, biting my lip. "There's no chance that this will spread to my abuelitos or anyone else in my family, is there? I wouldn't want anything bad happening to them. This is terrible enough for me and Keisha."

Pipo shrugs. "The Luck Eater wouldn't be mad at your abuelitos."

Eyebrows raised, I glance at Pipo. "Why not?"

He purses his lips. "Well, other than the fact that they actually burned their effigies, they have enough sadness to satisfy him."

I pause at the entrance of Zaragoza Park and put my hand on the low stone wall, its rocks bleached by the sun and weathered by the salty wind. Several people stand on the pier stretching out from the park as waves beat against the pilings, sending foamy spray into the air.

"Are they really that sad?" I ask Pipo, thinking of Abuelita's face as she rested her head on Abuelito's shoulder when the effigies burned. My voice gets carried away by the breeze playing in the branches of the live oak trees.

The wind flips my hair in my face, but it has no effect on Pipo's. "There's sadness that sits high in your throat," he says. "It comes out in everything you say and pushes tears out of your eyes. Then there's sadness that sits low in your belly. It makes itself comfortable. Sometimes you even forget it's there. But if you move just right, your muscles ache and the pain burns in your chest. Your abuelitos may not always show their sadness. But it's there."

I bite my lip. "Are you . . ." I pause, unsure what I really want to ask. Scuffing my foot in the grass as a sandpiper scurries away, I take a deep breath. "Are you the reason why my abuelito is sad?"

Pipo motions for me to sit on the stone wall. I hop up and tuck my hands in the pocket of my hoodie. The mark on my arm tingles like a colony of fire ants are crawling across it.

"Your abuelito was fifteen when I left. The day before I flew to the United States, we spent the morning on the beach in Matanzas. We fished from this little wooden boat I had and cooked tarpon right on the shore. I told him I was going to ask Eugenia to marry me once I got back, and he said he'd rather kiss a fish on the lips."

I smile. I've never heard anything about what Abuelito was like when he was around my age.

"I was gone for a year, training and thinking about our mami's arroz con leche the entire time. I couldn't write to Nano, because no one could know where we were or what we were doing. The next time I set foot on my island, I had a rifle in my hand and sand in my boots. I never got to see Nano again."

I want to put my hand on Pipo's shoulder. I notice tears glistening like diamonds and pooling in the corners of his eyes.

"Are you sorry you did it? I mean, are you sorry you tried to fight?"

Pipo shakes his head. "I'm not sorry for trying to keep my family safe or for trying to make my country better. But I am sorry I didn't get to watch Nano grow up. He was my best friend."

I smile and tuck a loose strand of hair behind my ear. "He's pretty much the best abuelito ever, if that helps. He sings songs with me, he has pastelito-eating contests with me, and he likes to annoy Liset as much as I do."

Pipo wipes his eyes as he smiles. Sitting down next to me, he says, "That doesn't surprise me at all."

We sit for a moment, watching the people in the park. Two kids stand next to the water, tossing nets into the waves to catch bait. I hear music, a swirl of violins and trumpets, and search for whoever brought a speaker. But there are only a few men playing basketball, a handful of kids riding scooters, and a group of old people sitting in lawn chairs, watching the waves. No speaker in sight. I look down and see Pipo tap his fingers on his leg to the rhythm of the music. He swirls his fingers in the air, and the trumpets run a fast scale. He grips his fingers into a fist, and the music stops.

My eyes grow wide. "Were you doing that? Making the music?"

Pipo chuckles. "Being dead has its advantages. I get to play music anytime I want."

I tap my fingers on my leg and wiggle my fingers in the air, but the only sound we hear is the squawk of a brown pelican as it soars above us.

"That's so cool," I say. "Is speaking fluent English another advantage, or did you learn that before you died?"

Pipo raises an eyebrow. "What are you talking about?"

"Your English. It's way better than Abuelito's."

He slaps his leg and laughs. "I couldn't speak a word of English before. What's funny is that in my head, I'm speaking Spanish when I talk to you."

"That's weird."

"But not the weirdest thing out of all of this, no?"

Thinking for a moment, I consider Pipo's ability—how he can make music appear out of nowhere. I heard violin music last night, and music filled the yard right before Pipo appeared when I tried to burn the effigy. The music had been the sign that he was coming all along.

All the drips I heard in school led up to Andaluz appearing in the bathroom, but thinking about that makes me shudder.

I nod at Pipo and wipe my glasses on the bottom of my hoodie. Ramming them back on my face, I square my shoulders and hop down from the wall. "Okay," I say to Pipo. "Let's convince my friends that this Luck Eater nonsense is real and figure out a way to stop it."

Pipo smiles. "Deal."

My tío abuelo and I head into the park and look for Keisha. She'd texted before I left my house to tell me she'd be practicing there, her coach not so quietly asking her to leave training after her metal fencing foil went inexplicably as limp as a spaghetti noodle.

I quickly spot her under an enormous live oak tree, lunging forward, no foil in her hand. She's wearing her white fencing jacket and her mask, a white raven head on the black mesh, painted by her mom.

And she's with Syed.

I groan. I don't want to deal with that on top of Keisha's being mad at me for her terrible fencing practices.

Before I reach Keisha and Syed, a voice calls out behind me. I turn as Juan Carlos jogs up to me and Pipo. I shift my weight from foot to foot, realizing I hadn't planned on explaining why I'm hanging out with a strange man in a city park.

"Hey," Juan Carlos says, eyeing Pipo warily.

I give him a weak wave.

Juan Carlos looks Pipo up and down and takes in his weathered boots, brown pants, and khaki shirt. "Who are you?"

I shove my hands into the pocket of my hoodie, pulling on the loose threads inside with my fingers. "So, this is Pipo Feijoo, my tío abuelo. He's my abuelito's brother."

Juan Carlos stares at Pipo's face, noticing the absence of wrinkles around his eyes, his straight posture, and his dark hair that's free of gray streaks.

"This guy is your seventy-year-old abuelo's brother?"

Pipo looks at me, and I nod. Clearing his throat, he says, "I died in 1961. You'd look young too if you were frozen as a twenty-two-year-old."

I watch as Juan Carlos chews on his lips, adjusting his glasses on his face. "When's your birthday?"

"November fourth, 1939."

"What's Mari's abuelito's favorite food?"

"Guava and cream cheese on water crackers."

"How'd you die?"

"I was executed in a Cuban prison."

Juan Carlos swallows hard. "Are you going to try to possess me?"

"I hadn't planned on it."

Juan Carlos nods. "Okay. Nice to meet you," he says, sticking out his hand.

Pipo reaches out to return the greeting, his fingers passing though Juan Carlos's hand. Juan Carlos's eyes grow wide. "Awesome."

"You're really okay with this, Juanito?" I ask.

He shrugs. "With everything that's been going on, all the bad luck you and Keisha are having because of some psycho possessed doll . . . this seems pretty normal."

"We'll figure out how to fix that," Pipo says.

When we reach Keisha and Syed, she stares at Pipo curiously.

"Um, this is something just the Super Ojos should talk about," I tell her, glancing at Syed. He looks at me with raised eyebrows and runs his fingers through his black hair.

Keisha presses her mouth in a tight line. "That's rude."

"Well, there's a lot going on that would be hard to explain," I shoot back, clenching my fists in my hoodie pocket.

Syed clears his throat. "No. She's right. It does seem like the Super Ojos have a lot to deal with right now," he says. "I hope y'all figure it out."

I know Syed hasn't said anything wrong—he's even agreeing with me—but all I can think of is Liset abandoning her friends the second some pimply boy looked at her. I'm not going to let that happen to the Super Ojos.

"*We* will," I say, crossing my arms.

Keisha rolls her eyes and starts to say something, but Syed swings his fencing bag over his shoulder. "I'll let y'all plan," he says. "I've gotta get home anyway."

He waves goodbye and jogs away through a group of kids who are flying octopus-shaped kites.

When I introduce Keisha to Pipo, she isn't as quick to believe me as Juan Carlos was. She hides behind the live oak tree, away from Pipo, after he shows her how he can pass his arm through my stomach. She squeezes her eyes shut and shakes her head.

"Nope. Not real. You guys are playing a trick," she mutters to herself.

Pipo stands behind me as I hold my hands out and say, "Keisha, he's here to help us. We figured out why everything is going wrong."

Keisha peers sheepishly from behind the tree. "How is he here? How is this possible?"

I hold out the diary and flip through the pages, showing Keisha and Juan Carlos where I wrote about Pipo, the words looking more like sheet music than neat paragraphs.

"That's actually because of me, too," I say, scuffing my feet in the grass, hoping they'll believe me. "It turns out I have a family . . . *gift*. I can . . . uh, make my dead relatives appear if I write about them."

I look from Keisha to Juan Carlos and bite my lip, waiting for their reaction.

Juan Carlos raises an eyebrow and whispers, "Freaking awesome."

I watch Keisha expectantly. She shoves her fencing blade into her bag and zips it up with more force than necessary.

Groaning, she says, "So not only are we dealing with a curse of bad luck, there are also ghosts now. Perfect."

I start to defend myself, but Keisha waves a hand and interrupts. "So what are we going to do about this bad luck and whatever's causing it? Because it needs to stop now."

"Well, the solution is easy. I've got it," Pipo says excitedly. "This is brilliant. We starve it."

Keisha jumps at his voice. "Who is 'it'?" she asks, looking at me instead of Pipo.

I clear my throat. "It's a luck eater. He takes all the sadness from the effigies for his food. When I didn't burn mine, we believe he decided to fill it up with as much bad stuff as possible. That's really why we're having bad luck. We think it's to get back at me for starving him."

Pipo puts his hands on his hips. "Exactly. So you can't let the things he does bother you. If you're not sad, there's nothing to fill up the effigy. The Luck Eater won't have anything to eat, and he'll give up."

Keisha, Juan Carlos, and I stand under the meandering branches of the live oak tree, thinking. Shorebirds circle over a group of women fishing from the pier, waiting to snap up their discarded bait. Finally, Juan Carlos speaks up.

"That's not normal."

"What?" Pipo asks.

"That's not normal, to not feel sad when something bad happens to you. If my skateboard bursts into flames or the crabs at the wildlife center snap off my toes, you better believe I'm gonna be sad. I'm gonna cry like a baby. No shame."

"But nothing is happening to you," Keisha snaps.

Juan Carlos starts to speak, but I interrupt. "Juan Carlos is right. What if it takes forever for the Luck Eater to decide we're not worth it? We've already had enough, with all this bad luck piling together, and it's barely been a week. We need to come up with something else."

Keisha clears her throat and finally looks at Pipo. "I have to practice. Things can't keep messing up."

Pipo shrugs. "Well, it seemed like a good idea."

I give Pipo a weak smile. "It makes sense, and I think we could probably try to do it as much as we can, to prepare for whatever the Luck Eater might throw at us, but we need something more permanent."

Pipo taps his fingers on his lower lip, deep in thought. "Like what?"

Keisha, Juan Carlos, and I stare at each other.

We've got nothing.

Feeling defeated, we walk away from the park, discussing the best ways to prepare for Luck Eater tricks. As I glance back, I see a shadow creep from behind the live oak tree. Maybe it's just the strong Texas sun, but the figure looks like it has scales.

And maybe it's just the gulf breeze, but I swear I hear laughing.

ELEVEN

PIPO FADED AWAY after I got back to my house. One minute he was following me on the sidewalk, the next minute all I could see were his boots slowly disappearing into the concrete.

It was just as well. His idea to defeat this Luck Eater thing wasn't that great. And if Abuelita saw him, she would've screamed loud enough for the entire neighborhood to hear while she tried to beat Pipo away with a wooden spoon.

On Monday, thick dark clouds hang over the school and a flock of crows line up on top of the roof, looking like they're waiting to see what new torture the Luck Eater has waiting for me.

At least the Super Ojos are prepared.

"Juanito, how heavy is your backpack? It looks like you're smuggling a dolphin," I say as I join Keisha and Juan Carlos after lunch. My stomach growls. I couldn't eat my sandwich at lunch. One glance, it would look fine, but when

I'd look again, the bread would turn a fuzzy dark green while fat maggots squirmed from the filling. I decided to trust my eyes, and I threw it in the trash.

The three of us had convinced Ms. Faruqi to let us work in the hallway, claiming that the classroom noise made it impossible to think. Truthfully, it was partly the noise, partly because I was tired of watching the markers on the whiteboard turn into slugs and inch toward my feet. I didn't want everyone to look at me when I screamed because the top of my desk erupted into flames, like I thought it had in Mr. Nguyen's class. But best of all, working in the hallway means I get away from any new comments from Mykenzye.

I tried to ignore her when she made a point of asking me in front of the entire class if my parents spoke English. I wanted to yell that there was nothing embarrassing about learning a new language or having parents who didn't speak English, even though mine did. But Mykenzye wouldn't care.

"No dolphin," Juan Carlos says as he unzips his backpack, revealing the contents. "But it has everything you need, including a change of clothes in case either of you need it today. Also plastic bags for clothes that get covered in spoiled chocolate milk or whatever. I have a new toothbrush and toothpaste in case that Luck Eater makes anything taste like dog poop. And some foam plugs for your noses for when the air conditioner spews gorilla farts on you. We're set."

He gives Keisha a sheepish look, but she ignores him, her gaze stuck on her notebook. She's said less and less lately, glaring at her arm every time she scratches the mark. I get why she's mad. She knows I don't like Syed butting in to the Super Ojos, but piling on a curse and bad luck on top of that is probably too much for her.

I've got to make it right.

I nod at Juan Carlos and play with the black beaded bracelet around my wrist. I'd asked Mami to find the azabache I had as a baby. It was supposed to keep away the evil eye. Mami was confused, but she managed to find the bracelet in my baby book, tucked between photos of me face-deep in my first birthday cake while I sat on Abuelita's lap.

Maybe this Peak Cubanity will actually help.

Keisha mumbles under her breath, "So what's the score today, Mari?"

She settles down in the hallway, her back to the wall, only after inspecting it for spiders or wet paint. Her nails are completely gone, and she has bandages around the tips of three fingers.

As I open my notebook to a clean page, a thick brown cockroach scurries toward me and I kick it away quickly. "Well, I knew the bus would ignore me again, so I made sure my bike was ready to go. I brought money for lunch in case the sandwich I made turned to black mold. Which it did. Thankfully, I don't have mariachi practice after school, so at least nothing can go wrong there. And I'm on letter *G* of my Insult Dictionary about this Luck Eater."

Juan Carlos thinks for a moment. "They're a gross grimy goblin."

He looks at Keisha expectantly, but she just looks away.

Juan Carlos shrugs and keeps going. "A hairless hideous hangnail."

I bite my lip and think for a minute, then say, "Okay, *I*. Got it. An ignorant idiotic iguana."

Juan Carlos chuckles and hugs his backpack. Another cockroach creeps out from under Ms. Faruqi's classroom door. Juan Carlos squashes it with his notebook and smirks, glancing at his backpack. "Thanks to Señor Listopatodo here, we're ready for anything. What about you?" he asks Keisha cautiously.

Keisha twirls her pencil between her fingers and raises her eyebrow. "Well, my fencing bag has three kinds of screwdrivers and tape, in case my glasses break, duct tape to keep my glove on, and a small fire extinguisher in case my blade decides to shoot sparks again. I don't think my moms' eyes could've gotten any wider when I asked for a spatula and a first aid kit."

"Why would you need those?" I ask.

"The spatula is to pry my mask off my head when it gets stuck. And the kit is for when the rubber tip on my opponent's foil falls off and I get stabbed in the gut."

"Yikes. Hopefully it won't get that bad," I say, only a little relieved that Keisha is talking this much again. "We just need to make it through the day, and then, after school, we'll figure out how to stop this Luck Eater. For good."

Out of the corner of my eye I spot two more cockroaches scurrying down the hall toward us. I pull my knees to my chest as they stop three feet from us, pointing at us with their antennae.

Keisha chuckles but doesn't sound like she thinks anything is funny. She clearly doesn't notice the bugs. "Are we gonna ignore the fact that we're working with a ghost? Like everybody's just cool with that?"

Juan Carlos shrugs, holding his backpack closer. "And here I thought the worst thing about sixth grade was gonna be having to deal with the tiny toilets meant for kindergartners in the bathroom. I did not expect to have Mari's dead relative or some Luck Eater dude in the game."

I shove Juan Carlos in the arm and laugh. "Hey, at least Pipo showed up. I'm glad I wrote about him in my diary."

"Yeah, but now what? He didn't exactly come up with a brilliant plan," Keisha says. She clenches her pencil like it's one of her fencing blades.

We sit in silence as Juan Carlos looks at me and shrugs. I take the diary out of my backpack and flip through it, unsure what to do.

The cockroaches in the hallway have disappeared, but when I look at the large window across the hall, it's covered with an unusually large number of black flies. I swallow hard and blink, hoping it's just another twisted vision.

Juan Carlos clears his throat. "So do you think you can write about anyone in there? And they'd show up?"

I turn to the page where I'd written about Andaluz, the words faded and gone. "It seems like it."

"Well, maybe we just need to try someone else in your family. Maybe another Feijoo will have a better idea."

Keisha groans. "This is so weird."

My stomach flip-flops. I'm used to Mykenzye thinking everything I do is strange. Keisha has never thought that. She's always been by my side. But maybe my Peak Cubanity is too much for her now.

I don't know how to respond to Keisha, so we all settle in and work on our world fair projects. Juan Carlos has to redirect my attention every time someone walks past us in the hallway, and I eye them warily, scooting closer to him and Señor Listopatodo. The number of flies on the window have increased, buzzing over the glass and almost blacking out the view outside.

The squawk of the birds increases and the flies disappear from the window. As we bend over our notebooks, the hallway light above us flickers and turns off with a pop.

"Oh, no. What now?" Keisha says as a light farther down the empty hallway snaps off, the sharp crack echoing on the tile floor.

"I've got this. Señor Listopatodo has a flashlight," Juan Carlos says, rummaging in his backpack.

Like dominoes cascading, the hallway lights flick off one by one all the way to the front door. A bolt of lightning flashes outside, bathing us in a harsh glow for a brief second and revealing a figure standing in the open doorway of the school. The man is hunched over, his shoulders heaving as he braces his thin arms on the doorframe.

I blink several times, wondering if what I'm seeing is real.

Keisha points down the hallway with a shaky finger. "Who . . . who is that?"

And then the man opens his eyes.

Black abysses swirl as bright green light takes over and shines from his face. My stomach clenches, and I think I might throw up. The glow from the man's eyes lights up his face, revealing long, jagged teeth frozen in a sneer. His skin is scaly under his stringy black hair.

Juan Carlos drops his flashlight and grabs my arm,

his nails digging into my skin as his hand shakes. "Is that the . . . the Luck Eater?"

The man raises his chin, barely moving his mouth, and a slithering sound snakes down the hallway toward us.

"Yes."

I shiver. A heaviness in my chest chokes the breath from my lungs. I grab Keisha's hand, and she squeezes my fingers until my knuckles crack. The mark on my arm feels like someone is holding a lighted match to my skin. Keisha winces and shakes her arm. Her mark must feel the same way.

The man takes one step forward into the school as lightning flashes again. He doesn't cast a shadow across the tile. He lifts his arm and points a boney finger at us as we scoot across the floor, away from the doorway, too afraid to stand.

"Why, hello, Mari. So nice to finally meet the youngest Feijoo," he says, his voice sounding dead in the hallway. "And when no other pesky family member is around to push me back, like that drenched girl and that foolish soldier."

The man clenches his fists, his sharp nails digging into his palms, leaving droplets of black blood on the floor.

"How does he know you?" Juan Carlos whispers, but I can't answer.

The man's lip curls in a sneer. "I'm afraid I have bad news about all your little preparations. You can't win against me," he says, taking a deep breath. His chest heaves, as if speaking requires all his energy. "And do you know why? Because, even though I need your sadness to fill up the effigy, I found one special bonus. Your fear is too delicious."

In an instant, the man shoots toward us, tumbling down the hall, his teeth bared, his bloody hands stretched out.

We scramble away from him, a tangle of limbs unable to stand and run. We yelp and whimper as the man grows closer and closer.

Just before he's within reach, just before he can scratch my skin with his long nails, the classroom door swings open, blocking his path.

"Making a little too much noise out here, kids," Ms. Faruqi says, standing over us.

We blink as the hallway lights snap back on. The figure behind the door is gone, the only evidence of his existence a bloody handprint on the wall that slowly drips down to the floor.

TWELVE

ON OUR WAY to my house after school, we barely speak, still too shaken from what happened in the hallway. I chew on my nails as Keisha completely unravels the bottom hem of her shirt, nervously pulling on threads. Juan Carlos picks off every scab on his knuckles.

The waves pounding on the beach usually calm me. I make up melodies in my head that go along with their rhythm. But I can't hear them now. The only sound in my ears is the Luck Eater's snarl.

"Diapers."

I shake my head, snapping myself from my thoughts. "What'd you say, Juanito?"

"Diapers. I have to pack diapers in Señor Listopatodo if things like that are going to happen," Juan Carlos says, shuddering.

The seabirds flying above squawk as they watch us hurry down the sidewalk to my house. We huddle together and look around every corner for a shadowy man in black. When we reach the front door, our sighs of relief fill the living room. Passing through the kitchen, I grab a handful of ajonjolí candies to share with Keisha and Juan Carlos. We find my abuelitos in the backyard, arguing over a mango that has fallen from a tree.

"Hi, Abuelitos!" I call, hoping my voice covers the uneasy feeling that still swirls in my stomach. I open an ajonjolí candy, popping it into my mouth, but the sticky sesame taste doesn't make me forget the sourness of school.

"Ay, mi vida," Abuelito says, smiling and inviting me in for a big hug. I let the softness of his guayabera shirt surround me, and I breathe in the scent of his oaky cologne.

I look across the yard to the metal firepit where we burn effigies on New Year's Eve, and I spot a small piece of partially burned green fabric sticking out of the ashes, a remnant of Papi's effigy.

"¿Y la escuela? ¿Cómo les fue?" Abuelita asks as Abuelito releases me. I sit down with Keisha and Juan Carlos on the steps of the patio and pass an ajonjolí to each of them.

Keisha inspects the candy closely before popping it into her mouth. "School was . . . interesting," she says.

"Por supuesto que es interesante. Hay tanto que aprender," Abuelita shoots back, her hands on her hips.

I shake my head. "That's not what Keisha means. Of

course, there's a lot to learn. But that's not what made today interesting. There's just some weird stuff going on that we're trying to figure out."

I'm not sure how to explain it in a way that won't make my abuelitos think I'm one domino short of a full set.

Keisha speaks up before I can. "So, um, Mr. and Mrs. Feijoo, do you think we could ask you some questions about Cuba? It's for a school project."

Juan Carlos raises his eyebrow at Keisha, and she shrugs her shoulders, a determined look set on her face. I tug at the edge of my hoodie. My abuelitos never talk to me about what happened in Cuba, but maybe they'll tell Keisha and Juan Carlos.

"You all present Cuba?" Abuelita asks. She looks at each of us, and her eyes stop on me. I squirm.

"Sure," I say, scuffing my feet on the wood slats of the patio deck. I don't like lying to my abuelitos, but I don't see any other way. Pipo said that calling on the dead was a family trait, but I've never seen my abuelitos do such a thing. I can't tell them I'm trying to make the ghosts of more relatives appear to help me because I've been cursed by the Luck Eater.

That's not Peak Cubanity.

That's Peak Insanity.

Abuelito shouts loudly, making us all jump. "¡Así es! Sabía que eran los más inteligentes de todos."

Juan Carlos laughs, and Keisha turns to me so I can explain.

"My abuelito says we're the smartest out of everybody for picking Cuba," I say.

Keisha smiles softly and gives Abuelito a shy wink. "I'm okay with that."

"What you need to know?" Abuelita asks, sitting at the patio table with Abuelito.

I take a deep breath and drum my fingers on my knee. Pulling my diary out of my backpack, I try to decide how to get Abuelita to talk about family members who might help us with the Luck Eater.

"So, we could present all these facts about Cuba, but we thought that would be pretty boring. I thought if I talked about family, that would make Cuba a little more real to everybody."

I look at my abuelitos warily. I don't want to upset them by making them talk about something they want to avoid.

Abuelita smooths her hands on her skirt. "Bueno, you want to know about family?"

She pauses and looks out into the yard, watching the green jays peck at another fallen mango. The birds pick at the orange flesh, and my eyes widen when short, fat worms pour from the fruit.

Maggots.

I look at Abuelita, but it's obvious that she doesn't see

the same thing as I do. I squeeze my eyes shut, shake my head, and try to focus on getting the information I need.

I clear my throat, wracking my brain. That's when I remember.

"When you gave me my diary for New Year's, you were looking at your Bible, and I saw the family tree in it. There was one name that stuck out—Fautina. Is that where Liset got her middle name from?"

Abuelita twists her hands in her lap, still staring off into the yard as thick clouds float overhead. For a moment, I'm afraid she's going to change her mind and not say anything. That she'll come up with a sudden chore she has to do in the kitchen and leave us stranded in the backyard.

"Ay, she is my abuelita like I am yours," she finally says. "She make the best arroz con pollo."

"Abuelita, you make the best arroz con pollo," I say, my voice shaking. She's oblivious to the maggots squirming out of the mangos and into the grass. Past the mango trees, on the wooden fence that borders our yard, I notice red marks seeping out of the slats. Squinting, I recognize what they are.

Bloody handprints inching toward the firepit.

Juan Carlos looks at me and raises an eyebrow, but I shake my head. We have to keep going. I know we're onto something. Something that the Luck Eater is trying to stop us from getting.

"Who you think I learn from? She teach me tostones, croquetas, picadillo, frijoles, flan . . . all the best food," Abuelita responds. A grin spreads over her face. It's the first time I've seen her smile when she talks about someone she left behind in Cuba.

Abuelito pats his belly and chuckles. "Gracias, Santa Fautina."

"So she was a pretty good cook?" Keisha asked. "She probably would've gotten along with my grammie."

Abuelita nods at Keisha, as if energized by our interest in Fautina's food. "Claro. But she not only cook. She tell stories. She tell me all about our family. All they do, who they are. The best stories. So real. Like picture on television."

Juan Carlos looks at me and nods. Keisha scrawls everything Abuelita says in her notebook.

It sounds like Fautina might have been able to do what I can do.

The wind picks up in the yard, ripping Keisha's paper out of her notebook. It shoots across the yard toward the firepit.

"Get it!" Juan Carlos yells.

We all jump up, chasing after the paper as it sails through the grass.

Keisha reaches the paper first as it lands in the firepit. I come up behind her and reach between the ashes and blackened twigs for the page, but just as my fingers touch it, the paper bursts into flames.

"Mari, look out!" Juan Carlos says.

I pull my hand back and clutch my fingers. The paper is consumed in flames until it's nothing but gray ash.

"How . . . how is that possible?" Keisha stammers.

"Because we're close. I can feel it. The Luck Eater is trying to stop us," I whisper to Keisha and Juan Carlos.

Looking across the yard to the back fence, I'm proved right. Because the bloody handprints are gone. Instead, uneven red writing over the knobby wood taunts me.

NICE TRY.

THIRTEEN

THE NEXT DAY at school, Juan Carlos is armed with an overstuffed Señor Listopatodo. I resist the urge to ask him if it's stocked with diapers.

I grip my new backpack, Señorita Por Si Las Moscas. Abuelita always tells me to pack more pairs of underwear than I need when we travel, por si las moscas. She makes extra pastelitos, por si las moscas. She carries a small umbrella in her purse even when it's sunny, por si las moscas.

Just in case.

Last night, I wrote about Fautina in my diary, managing to remember everything Abuelita said, even though Keisha's notes burned up in the firepit. But now, after a day at school where quivering slugs covered my seat in all my classes, every paper I wrote turned into fluttering white moths right before I'd hand it in to my teacher, and the cafeteria chicken nuggets morphed into shiny black beetles, I walk around town with Keisha and Juan Carlos, unsure of what else to do. Fautina hasn't appeared yet.

I notice dark spots under Keisha's eyes and her nails completely bitten off. She barely talks, and she looks away whenever I make eye contact. We've been friends since kindergarten and have always had something to say to each other. I think I hate the Luck Eater the most for this.

"You're certain she hasn't shown up?" Juan Carlos asks.

I roll my eyes. "I think it would be pretty obvious if another ghost relative appeared. And I'm starting to run out of ideas for my Luck Eater Insult Dictionary."

"What letter are you on?" Juan Carlos asks.

"*M.*"

He chews on the side of his mouth and thinks. "Hey, Luck Eater, you're a moldy microwaved mammoth."

"No, he's a microscopic muddy meatball," Keisha whispers. Juan Carlos and I look at her, but she stares at her shoes.

"So now what?" Juan Carlos asks.

I scratch the mark on my arm as it tingles. "Okay, I've been thinking about something. When I write about my family in the diary, the words change. And they usually change to show how the person is gonna appear."

"What are you talking about?" Keisha says, a bite in her voice that makes the mark on my arm hurt even more.

"What I wrote about Pipo looks like sheet music now,

and that fits, because he can play music anytime. And, uh . . . Pipo wasn't the first family member I got to appear. I wrote about my abuelita's cousin Andaluz in the diary too. She drowned trying to cross the Florida Straits between Cuba and the US."

The hard line of Keisha's mouth softens.

"When I wrote about her, the letters swirled like they were being soaked. And Andaluz ended up creeping out of a stall in the school bathroom after I heard water dripping everywhere."

Juan Carlos gasps. "So what about Fautina? Did anything happen to what you wrote?"

I pull the diary from my backpack and show them Fautina's page. The words have turned into a rainbow of colors. A drawing of a large dish filled with arroz con pollo sits at the bottom of the page. Directly underneath what I wrote, a picture of a small child wrapped in a blue blanket pops up.

Juan Carlos eyes the page closely and bites his lip. "So these pictures appeared when you wrote about her?"

I nod and push my glasses up the bridge of my nose. When I do, I hear a snap, and the lenses fall from my face and onto the sidewalk, followed by my green frames. When I pick them up, the earpieces detach from the front, and my glasses crumble into five pieces.

I groan and mumble, "Por Si Las Moscas to the rescue, I guess."

Tossing the destroyed glasses into my backpack, I pull out a lens case with an old pair of glasses. The prescription isn't quite right anymore, but it's better than nothing.

"Done?" Keisha says, crossing her arms and tapping her foot on the sidewalk.

I roll my eyes at her. Can't she see I'm trying to make things better? "Well, excuse me for being cursed by—"

"Okay, anyway," Juan Carlos interrupts. "I think I have an idea about Fautina. Maybe we need to give a storyteller an audience." He twists his lips, thinking. "We should go to the wildlife center. They have a story time there. And, well, despite being a scientist, Dr. Younts is actually into . . . dead stuff."

I raise an eyebrow. "What do you mean?"

Juan Carlos shrugs. "She's always talking about the jellyfish auras, and she did a tarot card reading for a sea turtle. She might know more about getting dead people to appear. Maybe she'll know how to help Fautina appear faster."

Keisha shakes her head. "My moms told me not to mess with stuff like that."

"Yeah, my abuela calls that cosas del diablo," I add.

Juan Carlos sighs. "So we're not supposed to do 'devil stuff,' but you've already summoned two of your ghost relatives and we've gotten the caca scared out of us by some horrifying Luck Eater?"

He turns down the sidewalk and hurries toward the wildlife center, calling over his shoulder, "Way too late, Super Ojos!"

The Port Ballí Wildlife Center sits tucked between rows of royal palm trees, the limestone building weathered by the salty gulf air. Juan Carlos guides us through the large glass doors, past huge tanks filled with blue and yellow striped pinfish, silvery pink Atlantic croaker, and fat brown catfish.

When I pass a tank of spotted sea trout, one fish raises its head to the surface and spits a long stream of water right in my face.

"What the frijoles? Come on!" I yell, wiping my old glasses on the edge of my shirt, hoping these lenses stay put. I yank a red rain jacket out of Por Si Las Moscas and put it on.

We venture to the back of the wildlife center, entering a room filled with bubbling tanks. Our shoes squeak as we walk across the rubber mats on the wet concrete floor. Juan Carlos ushers us to the back of the room where there's a long table under warming lights. A blond woman stands counting sea turtle eggs, her blue eyes darting over trays as she scribbles on a clipboard.

"Dr. Younts? Could we talk to you for a minute?" Juan Carlos asks.

The woman sets her clipboard down on the table and

eyes me and Keisha. "I didn't see you on the schedule today, Juan Carlos. Which is good, I think. Fewer people to bore with your endless animal facts, I suppose."

I purse my lips at Dr. Younts and cross my arms. Keisha mutters under her breath, "Excuse you."

Keisha and I may not be getting along that well right now, but no one messes with the Super Ojos.

"Uh, yeah, right," Juan Carlos answers. "Sorry about that. Stuff just comes out of my mouth sometimes."

"You don't need to apologize for being excited about something, Juanito," I whisper to him.

The light above us pops and cracks, its electric hum filling the room. The slithering eels in a tank along the far wall slap their tails on the glass, the sound echoing off the wet floor.

"What do you need?" Dr. Younts asks. She walks over to a cage of mud crabs and tosses in a handful of oysters. The mud crabs attack the oyster shells with their black pincers, ripping them apart and feasting on the flesh inside. Dr. Younts's thin lips curl at the sight.

"Make it quick, Juanito," I whisper. "I'm getting a bad feeling about being here."

Keisha nods, pressing herself against my shoulder.

"Right," Juan Carlos says, clearing his throat. "So, Dr. Younts, this may seem a little weird—"

"That would be expected from you," Dr. Younts

interrupts. She picks up her clipboard again and runs a dark green painted nail along the edge.

"Oh, no. She didn't . . ." Keisha says, digging her fingers into my arm.

"Yeah, uh, okay." Juan Carlos fidgets and shoves his hands into his pockets. The baby alligator in the tank next to him snaps its jaws and hisses, making us jump. "I was wondering, since you seem to know a lot about this kind of stuff, if you could tell us how to . . . uh . . . summon dead people?"

Dr. Younts arches an eyebrow to a sharp point and purses her lips. She stares at Juan Carlos. "Really? Why? You must be getting desperate."

The laughing gulls on perches in the corner begin to squawk and beat their wings. Keisha and I edge closer together. The lights above us buzz louder, like a swarm of bees swirling the room.

"Well"—Juan Carlos rubs the back of his neck—"I just like learning new things, you know?"

Dr. Younts snarls and points a finger at him. Her green nails seem to have grown longer since we started talking. "Your silly skateboard tricks is learning something new. Your nose in a marine biology textbook is learning something new. This is on another level, even for you."

Juan Carlos takes a deep breath and steps forward. The mud crabs in the glass tank turn from the remnants of their oyster massacre and raise their pincers in the air, as if waiting for something else to shred to bits.

"But you really want to tell me, don't you?" A smile breaks out on Dr. Younts's lips. Instead of softening her face, it makes her teeth cast long shadows on her chin under the warming lights. "Oh, Super Ojos, Mari really has plunged you into quite the terrible situation, hasn't she?"

My stomach rolls as my spine starts to quiver. How does Dr. Younts know my name or that we call ourselves the Super Ojos? I've never met her before.

Dr. Younts plays with the crystal hanging around her neck, and it turns black under her fingers. The laughing gulls beat their wings again, their piercing calls ringing in my ears. The alligator huffs, its hot breath fogging the glass.

"And all because of her family's foolish traditions. You're right, Mari. That's the root of all your problems. Wouldn't it be easier to just ignore where you're from? It's just an island full of pain and sadness anyway." She reaches a hand toward Juan Carlos, and he takes a small step back. I jump as the mud crabs hit the glass of their tank, small cracks forming under their pincers.

"What are you talking about? How do you know all that?" I ask.

"Oh, I know you very well, Mari. One doesn't forget family."

Dr. Younts blinks, and her eyes glow green. She flashes a smile again, her teeth growing into jagged fangs. Her skin glistens and turns from a pale peach to an ashy gray.

Keisha gasps, and I yelp.

"You're . . . you're not Dr. Younts," Juan Carlos stammers.

The woman in front of us smiles again, cracked lips dotted with dark blood. She snaps her fingers, and the tank next to her explodes, mud crabs scurrying across the floor toward us. They grow larger with each frantic step they take.

Juan Carlos turns and pushes me and Keisha toward the door. He rips open Señor Listopatodo and takes out a small container.

"Hurry, Juan Carlos," I say, running down the hallway, away from the deep, cackling voice of Not Dr. Younts as the crabs nip at our heels.

Juan Carlos dumps out a container of brine shrimp, and the enlarged mud crabs stop in their tracks, gnashing and ripping the food apart.

Keisha pulls me and Juan Carlos through a door at the end of the hallway and slams it shut behind us.

We hunch over, our shoulders heaving as we catch our breath.

"Oh, hi there, Juan Carlos," a woman says, rounding the corner in the hallway.

Keisha grabs my arm and squeezes it. I look up and gasp.

"Hi . . . hi, Dr. Younts . . ." Juan Carlos stammers at the person standing in front of us who looks exactly like the woman we just ran away from. Except she doesn't have glowing green eyes, fangs, or scaly skin.

Dr. Younts raises her eyebrow. "You kids all right?"

FOURTEEN

"I . . . I THINK we're okay," Juan Carlos says, straightening up and catching his breath.

Keisha still holds on to my arm and examines Dr. Younts with narrow eyes.

I clear my throat. "Juan Carlos said you were the person to ask if we're curious about something," I say, my heartbeat still thudding in my cheeks.

Dr. Younts's eyes twinkle, and my breath calms down.

"I love curious people!" she says with a smile.

We walk with Dr. Younts down the hall, and I start to feel better as we get farther away from the Luck Eater and the snapping mud crabs. "I was wondering," I say to Dr. Younts. "Do you think it's possible to talk to dead people?"

I feel silly asking this. For me, the answer is an absolute yes.

"Oh, of course it is." Dr. Younts nods emphatically. "The dead speak to us in many ways."

"Sometimes right in your face in the middle of a park," Keisha mutters, and I poke her with my elbow.

"Well, is there a way to make it easier to talk to dead people?" Juan Carlos asks.

Dr. Younts opens a door and ushers us through into a meeting room filled with toddlers dragging their parents by the arm and shouting "Story time!"

She pauses and places a hand on her hip. "Certainly. The dead are attached to the objects of this world—things that were important to them, things that were precious. Think of family heirlooms or mementos. If you have something like that, it will be easier to communicate with whomever you are trying to contact."

I look from Keisha to Juan Carlos. I don't have heirlooms. My family couldn't bring anything with them when they left Cuba. Abuelito had one suitcase with one change of clothes. Abuelita came over with only the dress she was wearing. They had to leave everything behind.

I sigh, feeling defeated. Dr. Younts puts her hand on my shoulder, her eyes sparkling.

"Keep asking questions. Keep being curious. All the best people are!" she says with a wink before heading to the front of the room.

We're instantly surrounded by squirming toddler limbs as Dr. Younts announces that it's story time.

"Should we stay?" Juan Carlos asks.

Keisha nods. "We wanted to come to story time anyway. And I'm afraid if I walk too much right now, I might throw up in a fish tank."

We settle on the floor between a clump of nose pickers and a group of moms sneaking Goldfish to their kids despite the center's no-snack policy.

"So do you have anything in your family that's important, like Dr. Younts was talking about?" Juan Carlos asks.

Before I can explain, Dr. Younts makes an announcement. "We have a special guest today at the center, here to tell us a story from another land filled with sea creatures. I think you'll enjoy it."

A woman in a long purple dress with silver hair piled on top of her head in a loose bun appears from behind a fish tank and sits in a chair at the front of the carpet.

"Good afternoon, children. I'm so pleased to see all of you," she says. Her voice is velvet and soft, making me feel warm inside.

"Are we sure *that* woman is who she seems to be?" Juan Carlos asks. "I've never seen her at the wildlife center."

I swallow hard, but the glint in the woman's golden eyes calms my nerves.

"Are you ready for today's story?" the woman asks as the toddlers nod, squirm, and rock. One shouts that her dog just had four puppies.

The woman smiles. "Today's story is about three

fishermen. They were sailing in a small wooden boat across the sea to collect salt from a faraway bay."

The woman moves her arms, mimicking a rocking boat on the sea. Behind her, swirling blue waves appear and float across the bare wall of the room. Brightly colored fish dart in the water, swimming across the wall. I watch as a small brown boat pops up among the waves and floats in the water. Oohs and aahs erupt from the kids sitting on the carpet.

"As the three men traveled in their boat, a storm popped up, dark clouds hovered over them as rain pounded down, and the wind howled in their faces."

I watch in awe as the waves on the wall darken and thick black clouds appear. Birds squawk and fly away from the growing storm. The waves grow larger, and the small boat rocks up and down on the waves as the three men seated inside hold on to each other.

Keisha leans over to me and whispers, "How is she doing this?"

"Shhh," Juan Carlos says, his mouth hanging open and his eyes glued to the wall.

I look at the kids watching the story and see that they've stopped squirming, their attention completely on the story the woman is telling. I search the ceiling for some sort of projection system that could be casting the pictures on the wall behind her. But there's nothing.

The woman continues, her golden eyes sparkling as she speaks. "As waves began to crash into the boat, threatening to sink it, the men held hands. As the rain pounded down, filling the boat with water, the men prayed. As the wind howled in their ears, they called for safety."

Keisha, Juan Carlos, and I stare at the storm on the wall as the boat rocks up and down. The men inside huddle together. I swear I hear a crack of thunder as the woman continues her story.

"Just when the men thought all would be lost, when they thought the waves would claim them and the water would envelope them, the sky cleared. The rain stopped and the wind calmed."

The bright light of the sun breaks out on the wall as the blue waves still and the boat floats calmly on the water.

"As the men looked across the sea, they spotted a single white bird floating on the waves. When their boat drew closer, they saw that it wasn't actually a bird at all. It was a statue."

The bird sitting on the waves behind the woman slowly begins to change shape. But before I can tell what it's changing into, the whole scene—men, boat, and sea—fades and disappears into the wall, leaving a blank canvas.

"Now, what do you think the statue was?" the woman asks the kids with a wink.

One boy immediately calls out "Brontosaurus," despite

his mom furiously whispering at him to raise his hand. Other answers of spaghetti, clowns, and "I have two brothers" break out from the group of toddlers.

The woman stands and smooths her skirt. "Well," she says, placing a finger on her lips. "I suppose there's no right answer, is there? It's just your imagination."

She winks again, and the children clap. They slowly leave the room, dragged by their moms and dads to over-feed the tanks of fish and terrorize the seabirds.

"That's not true," I say as Keisha, Juan Carlos, and I stand. "I know this story. It's Peak Cubanity. There's a right answer."

"What do you mean?" Keisha asks.

"The statue the men found was a statue of Our Lady of Charity. The patron saint of Cuba is La Virgen de la Caridad."

I watch as the woman approaches us, her flowing purple skirt swirling as she walks.

"That's correct," she says, smiling widely. "It's so good to see you, Maricela."

FIFTEEN

I SIT ON a bench outside Dulcita's Paleta Shop and stare at my great-great-grandmother. We walked with Fautina from the wildlife center, the gulf breeze tangling our hair as Fautina's silver bun stayed firmly planted on her head.

· "I'm glad you showed up." I examine Fautina's face closely. I see my abuela's golden eyes flecked with green and my dad's mouth that turns up more on the left side than the right when he smiles. I see family.

Fautina grins and lifts her chin to the white-capped waves tumbling on the beach, the sand they churn up turning the water milky brown. "I'm glad you called on me," she says. "I'm grateful to meet my great-great-granddaughter. Even though she's attracted quite the menace. How did that happen?"

Taking a deep breath, I launch into my explanation. I tell Fautina about the effigy on New Year's Eve and all the bad luck that followed. I explain how I learned I could summon my ancestors by writing in my diary, and how it made Andaluz and Pipo appear. When I get to the part about seeing the Luck Eater in the school hallway, I squeeze my hands together as Keisha picks at the sole of her shoe and Juan Carlos bites down on the wooden stick of his horchata paleta.

"You're certain he had scaly skin, glowing green eyes, and black clothes?" Fautina asks. As she speaks, a translucent form of the Luck Eater appears on the sand in front of us. Keisha yelps and scurries to the bench, sitting next to me as Juan Carlos scrambles up and wedges himself next to Keisha.

"Don't worry," Fautina says. "It's not really him. It's just my story."

I bite my lip and think for a moment. "So *you* were making all those images appear on the wall at the wildlife center when you told the fishermen story?"

Fautina nods. "Didn't your abuela mention that I was a storyteller?"

"Yes, but she never said you could do that. But that's how you . . . I mean, I think you're like me. Is that how you could summon our ancestors?"

Fautina chuckles, the light sound swirling in the breeze. "Yes. If I told a story about one of our relatives out loud, they would appear. How do you do it?"

I tug on the sleeve of my Houston Aeros hoodie. "If I

write about someone in a diary my abuelita gave me, our ancestors show up."

A smile stretches across Fautina's mouth. "I didn't think anyone in our family had the gift anymore. Once we left the island, I assumed it was gone. But it's still there, in your spirit, connecting you to where you are from."

I rub my hand over the mark on my arm. I think I've reached Peak Cubanity more than anyone in my family.

"After we die, the gift changes. Now I can make stories appear before your eyes."

I nod. "Like how Pipo can play music without any instruments and Andaluz can control water."

Juan Carlos chews on his paleta stick and mumbles. "I think I'd like to be able to talk to animals. That would be a cool power. But I'd rather be able to do it and not be dead too."

Keisha twists her shoelace around her finger. I wait for her to say something, but she purses her lips and sighs.

Fautina smiles. She reaches to pat me on the knee, but her hand passes right through my jeans.

"I'm never going to get used to this," Keisha says, shaking her head.

Fautina winks at her. "But this Luck Eater you describe," she says, pointing to the faint apparition that still stands on the beach. "I know who he is."

"You do?" I ask.

"He's El Cocodrilo."

Juan Carlos puts his head in his hands. "The Crocodile? That doesn't sound good. You know crocodiles can't chew. They just crush and swallow you whole. No thank you."

Fautina purses her lips. "He's a luck eater of the worst sort. Most luck eaters do humanity a favor, taking their sadness and regret so they can move on and hope for better. But this one, he's not like the others. He's cursed to be a luck eater. He must feed on the sadness of humans so he doesn't wither away to nothing. The more misery there is, the more he gets to eat."

The form on the beach looks at us huddled together and snarls.

"Um, ma'am?" Keisha mumbles. "Could you make him go away, please?"

Fautina waves her hand, and the Luck Eater disappears, ashes floating over the waves.

"So this Cocodrilo guy is cursed?" I ask. "What the frijoles did he do?"

Drumming her finger on her lap, Fautina sighs, takes a deep breath, and flips her hand at the gulf waves. "El Cocodrilo was ashamed of who he was. He always desired to be someone else, even if it hurt the people he cared about the most."

My eyes widen as I look out at the gulf. The waves slowly turn light green, the water's surface growing spiky, almost like long blades of grass. We watch as the sea disappears and a tall hill rises in front of us. The air fills with the smell of something acidic.

"Um, Señora? Should you be doing this where everyone can see?" Juan Carlos asks.

Fautina laughs. "Don't worry. This time it's only for you."

She continues. "In 1898, the United States fought a war with Spain and made Cuba the battlefield. Soldiers fought in our towns, on our hills, and in our harbors."

Keisha, Juan Carlos, and I watch smoke rise from the grassy hill as shouts and laughter fill the air. Men in navy blue jackets with United States flags on the sleeves sit around a fire, smoking cigars. Around a separate fire, several men in khaki pants and shirts are gathered. They pass the US soldiers drinks and food before retreating to their own circle. But one man in khaki stays with the soldiers, pouring them drink after drink and slapping them on the back.

Even though his skin is tan and not scaly, he has the same piercing black eyes as El Cocodrilo. One of the Cuban soldiers tries to get El Cocodrilo to join them at their fire again, but he sneers and waves a dismissive hand.

"Along with his best friend, El Cocodrilo was part of a group of Cubans who assisted the soldiers from the United States. He didn't fight, though, and was only responsible for making sure that the soldiers had ammunition and that their weapons worked properly. But he desperately wanted to be part of the US soldiers. He thought his fellow Cubans were beneath them and was embarrassed by his countrymen."

Fautina waves her hand, and the grassy hill changes, the smoke thickening as the ground is covered with charging soldiers. Men run across a field, yelling and pumping their fists. Pops and cracks fill the air, and I jump. Some of the men crumple to the ground, clutching their chests and bellies as blood seeps through the fabric of their uniforms.

Three men in khaki shirts and pants crawl low across the grass, dragging small wooden crates. They shove the crates at the men in blue uniforms who break them open and take out long, shiny bullets to reload their rifles.

El Cocodrilo clutches a wooden crate to his chest and quickly runs away from the soldiers, in the opposite direction of the fighting.

"One day, El Cocodrilo's cowardice and shame caused him to lose the person he cared about most," Fautina says. "His closest friend."

My jaw drops as I watch El Cocodrilo stand over a soldier sprawled on the ground, dark red blood flowing from the back of the soldier's head and seeping onto the grass. El Cocodrilo bends down, and I think for a moment he's going to help the fallen soldier. Instead, he quickly unbuttons the soldier's jacket and removes it from his body. He does the same with the soldier's boots, placing them on his own feet after kicking off his worn shoes. He slips his arms through the jacket sleeves and snatches the hat that has fallen a few feet from the soldier.

Another man in khaki—his friend, the same man who called El Cocodrilo to join him at the fireside earlier—waves his arms at El Cocodrilo, pointing to the soldiers fighting on the hill. El Cocodrilo shakes his head furiously and begins to run away, but not before a sharp crack pierces the air and his friend clutches his stomach as red liquid bursts from his shirt. He falls to the ground, and El Cocodrilo turns back and runs to him, cradling him in his arms, his hands stained with blood.

"He stole that dead soldier's uniform?" Juan Carlos says, shaking his head. "And he got his friend killed because of it. He really is a smelly chum bucket."

"We're on letter *N*. He's a noxious nasty nematode," Keisha shoots back.

"What happened to him?" I ask.

"He traveled back up the mountains and told everyone he fought in the Battle of San Juan Hill with President Roosevelt's Rough Riders. He drank and told his lies; he fought anyone who asked him what had happened to his friend. He drank more and bragged that he had killed scores of Spanish soldiers."

The grass turns brown and smooth as it fades into a dirt street meandering through a small town. El Cocodrilo stumbles out of a building, a large glass bottle gripped in his hand. He's still wearing the navy blue jacket from the dead soldier, the gold buttons undone, exposing his sweaty, hairy chest. He snarls and takes a long drink as he braces himself against a column outside the building.

"One night, it finally caught up with him."

I watch as El Cocodrilo shuffles behind the building to the banks of a churning river. He takes another long drink from his bottle and throws it into the water. His head hangs as he looks at the United States flag on his sleeve. He picks at it until the threads loosen, and he tears it from the fabric. Twisting his arm back, he takes off the jacket and launches it and the patch into the river. But he loses his footing and stumbles in, disappearing beneath the water. I tighten my grip on Keisha's arm as my breath quickens.

The scene slowly fades as the river settles into the reappearing gulf waves.

"Did they ever find his body?" Juan Carlos asks.

Fautina nods. "Yes, they did. And the sadness and despair in his heart seeped into the ground where he was buried. He festered in that cocoon, surrounded by all manner of insects crawling over him."

"Oh, that makes sense," I blurt out.

Keisha raises an eyebrow. "Why?"

I sigh, too tired to keep things from her. "I've been seeing a bunch of insects on the effigy Abuelita made. And other creepy-crawlies pretty much everywhere—cockroaches, flies, worms. If El Cocodrilo was covered in insects when he turned into what he is now, maybe bugs are his thing? That and turning into other people, it seems."

As expected, Keisha groans. "Perfect. Just perfect."

Fautina nods. "I think you're right. All those insects turned El Cocodrilo into what you saw at your school, a miserable creature feeding off the bad luck of others. Except now he enjoys the taste of sadness. It's not something necessary for his survival anymore. He craves it."

"That makes sense," Juan Carlos says, still chewing on his paleta stick. "Lots of insects pretend to be other things. Phasmids look like sticks, the patterns on butterfly wings mimic predator eyes, and leaf insects . . . well, it's pretty obvious what they look like."

I roll my head back and sigh. "Do you have any idea how to stop him?" I say to Fautina. "Pipo said we need to starve him so that the effigy won't fill up, but that would be impossible to continue for long."

Keisha and I stand, and Juan Carlos tosses his paleta stick into the trash can, wiping his hands on his jeans.

"Yeah. I'm running out of supplies for Señor Listopa-todo," Juan Carlos offers.

"And we have big stuff coming up that the crocodile guy

would really like to mess up," Keisha says. "I have a fencing tournament, and Mari has a mariachi band audition."

Fautina shakes her head. "My goodness, those are much too tempting for El Cocodrilo."

I remember something the fake Dr. Younts mentioned right before the tank of mud crabs exploded. "El Cocodrilo said something I don't understand. He said we're family. What did he mean by that?"

Fautina stands, twisting her hands together as her lips purse.

"It's true. His real name was Reinaldo Samuél Crespo. He was my father."

SIXTEEN

BEFORE I CAN question what Fautina told us, before I can let it sink in that the cause of all the terrible things of the past few weeks was a member of my own family, Fautina begins to fade. First, her purple skirt flows in the breeze until only the sidewalk remains. Then the silver bun perched on the top of her head disappears into the orange light of the setting sun. The last thing I see are Fautina's eyes gazing at me, the golden flecks sparkling until they vanish.

I rummage in my backpack and yank out the diary so I can write down more about her and make her reappear.

But I don't know anything new to write. My hand shakes over the page as my brain searches for something to say about a relative I never even knew I had.

"I'm sorry—" I stammer. "I don't know enough to make her come back."

Stomping her foot on the sidewalk, Keisha grumbles. "No offense, Mari, but your family is annoying."

I slam the diary shut. "I'm sorry, okay? How many times do I have to say it?"

My cheeks flush, and Keisha narrows her eyes at me. But I don't stop. What's been brewing deep in my gut boils over.

"I know this is my fault, and I'm sorry you got wrapped up in it, but I'm trying, okay? I'm trying to fix everything. And it doesn't help when you keep getting mad at me. Just go complain about me to Syed like I know you want to."

Keisha crosses her arms and seethes. "Mad at you? I'm more than mad at you. I'm furious! I have my fencing tournament this weekend. Am I just supposed to wait around for this crocodile guy to screw everything up for me? And I *knew* you were jealous of me and Syed!"

"Hah! Hardly," I shout, and roll my eyes.

Juan Carlos clears his throat. "Listen, uh—"

Keisha waves him off and points a finger inches from my nose. "Figure this out. The sooner the better, because my tournament is this weekend, and the way things are going now, it's guaranteed to be a disaster. It's the least you can do for messing up my life."

She stomps down the sidewalk before I can say anything else.

I drop my hands in defeat, clutching the diary. "I don't know what else to do. If I could snap my fingers and make this all go away, I would."

Juan Carlos pats me on the shoulder. "I know you would. The Super Ojos have been through worse, you know."

I shake my head. "Worse than being cursed with bad luck? I don't think so."

Juan Carlos bites his lip. "Okay, maybe you're right. But we'll figure this out."

He takes my hand and squeezes it.

Just as I'm about to agree with him, a line of fire ants march out of a crack in the sidewalk and make a hypnotic parade toward my ankle. I jump away as their writhing red bodies spell something out on the concrete.

I WIN.

On Saturday, I walk to the Port Ballí Community Center for Keisha's fencing tournament. Juan Carlos and I usually flood her phone with good luck text messages, but now I'm not sure if she wants us there at all. She's barely spoken to us since Tuesday.

Every time something went wrong—from her pen exploding in the middle of an English test to her slipping in front of everyone on greasy sloppy joes that had inexplicably spread across the floor, she'd glare at me—I was too busy dealing with ants crawling out of my violin at mariachi practice and biting my fingers to apologize for the hundredth time.

I meet Juan Carlos outside the community center, my eyes darting up and down the sidewalk out of habit. I search for things that may or may not be there, the tingling on the mark on my arm the only hint that El Cocodrilo is messing with my mind.

"I repacked Señor Listopatodo with everything I thought might help Keisha for her tournament," he says, showing me the backpack slung over his shoulder. I look at the bag's black fabric and see it covered with safety pins securing pieces of paper that read "Crocodiles Suck," "At least I can generate my own heat," and "Hooray for the extinction of El Cocodrilo."

"I've got Por Si Las Moscas ready too," I say, pointing to my own backpack. "A water bottle, in case hers tastes like pee. An extra towel if hers turns to sandpaper. About fifty extra hair ties."

"I packed diapers," Juan Carlos says.

"You can add us to the supplies," a man's voice says behind us.

I turn and see Pipo and Fautina standing on the sidewalk. Their shapes are almost entirely solid. Someone would have to stare at them for a long time to see the yellow flowers of the lantana bushes rustling behind them.

"It worked!" I shout, running up to Pipo and Fautina.

"What do you mean?" Juan Carlos asks. "What worked?"

I pull my backpack off my shoulder and open it. Taking out my diary, I flip to a page covered with my bad handwriting and show it to Pipo and Fautina. "I wrote down everything you told me about yourselves. All the stories, everything you said. That way I could call you here."

Pipo smiles, and Fautina looks over the page. My heart had been beating so fast when Fautina first vanished that I couldn't think of anything to write to make her come back. But once I got home, I filled a page, describing the way she told her story at the wildlife center and what she looked like sitting with us in front of Dulcita's Paleta Shop. And I wrote down everything I remembered about Pipo in Zaragosa Park.

"This is wonderful, my dear," Fautina says, winking.

Juan Carlos steps forward and looks at my notebook. "Um, I'm not sure how permanent a record that is when your handwriting looks like a blindfolded squid wrote it."

"Hey, don't hate on the handwriting. It gets the job done."

Pipo laughs as I shove the diary into my backpack. "So your friend has some sort of sporting event today?" he asks.

"It's a fencing tournament. A coach from Houston is coming to watch her, and he'll decide if she can join his team."

Fautina lowers her head. "This sounds like just the sort of thing El Cocodrilo would love to interfere with."

Juan Carlos and I nod. "Exactly. So we've got to try to stop him," I say.

We lead Pipo and Fautina to the community center, looking like two kids accompanied by their older brother and grandmother. We find seats on the bleachers behind where Keisha's team is warming up.

"So I guess we keep an eye out for El Cocodrilo?" Juan Carlos asks.

Fautina shakes her head. "Unfortunately, he can do all the damage he wants without us ever seeing him."

"That's so unfair," Juan Carlos says, hugging his backpack to his chest. He turns to me. "We're on R, right? What a repulsive radioactive reptile."

"And he could be anyone in this gym, just like he turned into Dr. Younts at the wildlife center," I say, rubbing my palms on my jeans.

Pipo grunts. "So no one here is safe? This isn't going to be easy."

Keisha sees us in the bleachers, and her eyes grow wide when they fall on Pipo and Fautina. Juan Carlos waves, and I give her a thumbs-up. She smiles half-heartedly and then waves to her moms, who are a few rows down in the bleachers, before sitting next to Syed on the bench.

"Is that the coach? The Houston Daggers guy?" Juan Carlos asks, nudging me and pointing to a mustached man two rows behind us who is sitting with an open notebook.

I shrug. "I think so. He looks serious."

Pipo leans closer to me. "But is that really the coach? And not the other guy?"

Squinting, I examine the man as he watches the fencers prepare for their bouts. He doesn't have green nails like the fake Dr. Younts had, but I can't tell if the tight line on his lips is from concentrating on his evaluations or because he's plotting ways to make Keisha's fencing blade turn into a snake.

We turn our attention to Keisha, getting ready on the mat. She puts on a silver bib over her white fencing uniform, pulls a cord from the electronic scoring system, and hooks it to the back of her bib. Her opponent, a ninth-grade boy almost a foot taller than she is, does the same. The bib will register when her opponent makes contact with her torso, scoring a point. Keisha's opponent tests his blade, pressing the tip to her chest. The scoring system lights up, and a buzzer sounds. Keisha presses her blade to the boy's scoring bib, but nothing happens. She inspects the metal clip attached to her blade, but it's fine.

Keisha's coach runs over to her with another blade, and she quickly plugs it into the cord running from the sleeve of her fencing jacket. When she tests it again on her opponent's scoring bib, a green light flashes and the buzzer sounds through the gym when she presses her blade to his chest.

"Does that normally happen?" Fautina asks, her eyes still meandering around the gym—to spectators on their cell phones, the electronic scoreboard with flashing lights, and the large speakers blaring music between bouts. I have to remind myself that the family tree in Abuelita's Bible said that Fautina was born in 1905.

I shake my head. "Not really. Keep an eye out for El Cocodrilo."

Pipo stands and brushes his hands on his pants. "I think I'll join that Houston coach as he watches. Just to be sure, you know?"

He walks across the bleachers and sits behind the Houston coach, eyeing the man carefully.

I clench my fists as Keisha's bout begins, my nails digging into my palms. I focus on the mark on my arm, as if any tingling is a clue that something terrible is about to happen.

Keisha holds her mask to her chest and salutes her opponent, the judge, and the spectators with her blade. She slips on her mask, rolls her shoulders, and, placing one foot in front of the other, lowers herself into a slight lunge.

"En garde. Ready. Fence!" the judge announces.

Keisha's opponent lunges at her, attacking her left side with his blade, but she blocks him with her own. She takes two quick steps forward, lunges, and stabs her blade into his collarbone. The scoring system buzzes loudly and echoes through the gym.

"Yeah, Keisha!" Syed shouts, clapping loudly.

Juan Carlos grabs my hand and yells a cheer for Keisha.

Keisha and her opponent center themselves on the fencing mats, and the judge again announces, "En garde. Ready. Fence."

Keisha takes a wide lunge forward with her right foot, aiming directly for her opponent with her blade, but her foot slips, and she loses her balance. She stumbles toward her opponent and into his blade, scoring a point against herself.

"That's okay. She'll still win," Juan Carlos says, squeezing my hand.

Keisha shakes her head and looks at the bottom of her shoe.

"Um, Juanito. Does Señor Listopatodo have anything for slippery shoes?" I ask.

Juan Carlos fumbles in his backpack. "I've got this. I totally got this."

He yanks out a pair of shoes that have sandpaper superglued to the bottom. "I asked Keisha's moms for some of her old fencing shoes so I could fix this up. They gave me a weird look for that."

"But how do we get them to her? We can't exactly walk up in the middle of the bout." I look at the fencing judge, who never takes his eyes off Keisha and her opponent.

"I believe it's my turn now to help," Fautina says. She

takes a deep breath and whispers, "There was once a colony of the most beautiful butterflies. Their wings were painted with every shade the human mind had ever concocted. They would flit and fly in swirls, attracting the attention of every eye."

My mouth drops open as I look toward the ceiling of the gym. Big butterflies with bright blue and orange wings float along the metal rafters with smaller yellow and red butterflies. They're chased by other butterflies with wings of the deepest purple I've ever seen. Every single person in the gym cranes their necks toward the ceiling, watching the butterflies dance and fly around. Several butterflies land directly on the noses of a handful of spectators while everyone else watches to see where the other butterflies will perch.

I nudge Juan Carlos with my elbow. "Now, Juanito. Do it now."

Juan Carlos grabs the fencing shoes and hurries down to Keisha, past the judge, whose eyes are glued to a bright orange butterfly flying closer and closer to his head. His lip curls and his gaze narrows, completely unamused by the insects. At least he's distracted.

Kiesha takes the shoes, kicks off her slippery ones, and passes them to Juan Carlos. Securing her feet in the sand-paper shoes, she gives me a thumbs-up.

"And just as quickly as they appeared"—Fautina

continues her story—"the butterflies disappeared out the window."

The swarm of butterflies captivating everyone finds an open window in the far corner of the gym and flies out in a swirling, colorful clump.

Everyone shakes their heads at the sight and murmurs about the butterflies, but the tournament continues as before.

"Let's hope this works," I say.

Keisha rolls her shoulders and gets into position again, scuffing her feet on the mat as if to make sure the shoes will stick.

"En garde. Ready. Fence," the judge calls.

Keisha and her opponent trade barbs, lunging at each other. Keisha keeps advancing, nearly backing her opponent off the mat before thrusting her blade into his chest and scoring a point.

She quickly scores three more points, her opponent shaking his head at her speed. She wins the bout, and Juan Carlos and I clap until our hands hurt.

After saluting her opponent and the judge with her blade, Keisha disconnects herself from the scoring system and gives us a thumbs-up before sitting next to Syed on the bench.

She used to sit with us between bouts.

We watch the next bout as Syed faces a high schooler who has impossibly long arms. Keisha's feet bounce up and down on the gym floor as she wipes her sweaty palms on her fencing pants, her mask tucked under her arm. She keeps stealing glances at the Houston coach in the stands.

I want to say something to her. I want to say I'm sorry and tell her I hope everything turns out okay. But then I see her fingers meander under her jacket sleeve and scratch the mark on her arm.

"Jeffries! You're up!" Keisha's coach calls when Syed's match ends with his victory.

Keisha trots to the mat and goes through her usual warm-up, but this time she scuffs her sandpaper shoes on the mat as she slips on her fencing glove.

Keisha's opponent for this bout is a girl much shorter than she is. After testing her blade, which thankfully works, Keisha salutes and pulls her mask over her face.

The judge raises his arm and begins, "En garde. Ready—"

Before he can say "fence," Keisha pulls off her mask, her eyes wide. She sucks in three large breaths, her hand pressing to her chest.

"Fencer, put your mask back on," the judge says, a sour look on his face.

I watch as Keisha shakes her head and inspects the inside of her mask. My stomach rolls.

Keisha nods to the judge and puts her mask on. Lowering herself in a lunge, she points her blade at her opponent.

"En garde. Ready. Fence," the judge says quickly.

Keisha flies at her opponent and strikes her in the chest as she runs past her. The moment the scoring system buzzes and flashes a green light, Keisha yanks off her fencing mask, her chest heaving as she sucks in air.

"He's here. He has to be," I mumble as I open my backpack and feel around inside.

Keisha scores two more points in the exact same way, running past her opponent as she stabs her in the chest. Each time, she flings off her mask and gasps for air, as if the mask suffocates her when she has it on.

By the fourth point, her opponent figures out Keisha's strategy and dodges Keisha's attack, stabbing her with her blade in the side as Keisha runs past. It's now 3–1.

Keisha pulls off her mask again, and the judge warns, "Fencer, you will be disqualified if you continue to take off your mask."

I notice Keisha suck in two huge breaths before pulling her mask on. I lean over to Juan Carlos and whisper, "I'm going to try something."

Juan Carlos nods, but he doesn't take his eyes off the bout as Keisha's opponent scores another point.

I pull out the effigy from my backpack, the moldy

fabric and frayed edges staring back at me as the pink flowers shift and swirl, giving the doll a hideous grin.

"What are you going to do with that?" Juan Carlos gasps.

I grip the effigy tightly. "I thought about what Dr. Younts said, how the dead are connected to objects. El Cocodrilo really needs this doll. It's filled with all our sadness from everything going wrong. The first time he appeared, he went for my backpack with these slimy lizards. I didn't know why then, but it's probably because the effigy was inside. He wouldn't let me destroy it either. So if something were to happen to it . . ."

I stick my finger under the thread of a loose seam and flick. The thread snaps, and part of the filling inside the doll peeks out.

"I just have to distract El Cocodrilo with this long enough so he leaves Keisha alone," I say, snapping another thread with my finger. I scan the gym for any reaction, but everyone is focused on Keisha's bout.

Juan Carlos eyes the widening hole in the seam of the effigy. "If only we could suck El Cocodrilo into the doll. He's miserable enough to qualify."

Keisha resets quickly and lunges at her opponent the moment the judge announces "Fence," but she is unsteady on her feet and leans right into her opponent's blade, scoring a point against herself. The bout is tied 3–3.

I nudge my finger under another thread and pull until it

snaps. I glance around the gym to see if anyone reacts. The Houston couch focuses on Keisha's match, the judge rolls his shoulders, and Syed shouts encouragement to Keisha.

I can't tell if anyone is reacting.

Soon the scoring system buzzes loudly again throughout the gym, announcing that Keisha's opponent has scored yet another point. Keisha's shoulders move up and down as she tries to suck in air. Her opponent needs only one more point to win the bout.

"Señora Crespo, didn't you say El Cocodrilo was consumed by his sadness and despair?" Juan Carlos asks.

Fautina purses her lips and nods. "Yes, he was. There wasn't a single drop of happiness in him."

Juan Carlos squeezes his hands into fists and stares down at Keisha on the mats. "If an effigy absorbs all bad things, wouldn't it make sense too that it would absorb something completely made up of sadness?"

I bite my lip and snap another thread loose on the effigy, but it's too late. Keisha stumbles forward after the judge calls "Fence," her opponent taking advantage of Keisha's lack of balance and thrusting her blade into her chest. Keisha yanks her mask off as the buzzer announces that she lost the bout.

She stares at the floor as she trudges to the bench where her coach and Syed are sitting. I watch as Keisha shows

Syed her fencing mask, shaking her head as her shoulders heave and sweat drips from her forehead.

"It's okay," Juan Carlos mutters. "As long as she doesn't lose her next bout, she can still make it."

I glance at the Houston coach, his lips in a tight line as he scribbles in his notebook. I nod in agreement, but so far Keisha has fenced against faulty blades, slippery shoes, and suffocating masks. I'm afraid to let my imagination run wild to think about what the next bout might bring.

A loud buzzer sounds in the gym, signaling the beginning of Keisha's last bout. I break two more threads on the effigy, hoping El Cocodrilo will turn his attention toward me and try to stop me, hoping he'll leave Keisha alone.

But it doesn't work.

Keisha's final bout, and her hope of earning a spot on the Houston Daggers team, ends with the cord from the electronic scoring system yanking her off her feet and pulling her backwards, her opponent running forward and scoring an easy point five times. We sit helpless as Keisha tries to scramble to her feet, only to be pulled back by the cord.

After the bout, Keisha slides her mask off and drops her blade in her bag. She bites her lip, her gaze glued to the gym floor as tears pool in her eyes.

To a casual observer, it looked like Keisha was just

unsteady on her feet, a young fencer too inexperienced to be fencing at this level.

I watch the judge approach her as she sits alone on the bench, and I assume he's going to give her words of encouragement. He leans forward and waves his hands, wafting air to his nostrils. As he breathes in deeply, his eyes glow green. A thin smile breaks out on his scaly face.

El Cocodrilo locks eyes with me and winks. He flicks a long black fingernail three times in my direction, and I hear a sharp rip as all the seams of the effigy completely snap and pull apart. The destroyed pieces fall to the floor.

"Oh, sweet Mari, did you think I still needed that? Why would I when I can just breathe in your misery directly from the source?"

SEVENTEEN

BEFORE ANY OF us can react, El Cocodrilo vanishes in a green mist. I shove the pieces of the effigy into the pocket of my hoodie and rush off the bleachers to where Keisha is cramming her fencing equipment into her bag, tears streaming down her face.

"I'm sorry," I tell her. "I don't know how to stop him."

Keisha doesn't look at me as she unzips her fencing jacket, yanks it off, and stuffs it in her bag along with her chest protector. Her eyes snap to the pocket of my hoodie, where part of the destroyed effigy peeks out.

"You brought that here?" she gasps. "Why would you do that? Why would you do something that would guarantee El Cocodrilo's showing up? You sabotaged me!"

"I didn't!" I shake my head furiously. "You know he was going to come no matter what we did. I thought I could distract—"

"No," Keisha interrupts, stomping on the gym floor. "I don't want to hear your excuses anymore. You always have excuses. And I'm done."

I open my mouth again to explain, to make Keisha understand. But I know it'll be useless. I've been apologizing for the last week, and it hasn't made a difference.

"What do you mean you're done?" I ask.

Slinging her fencing bag over her shoulder, she whispers to me in a shaky voice that barely carries in the gym. "You didn't want me to make the team. Because then I'd get to hang out with Syed more. You can't stand that I have other friends and not just the Super Ojos. Of course you wanted me to lose." She finally looks at me and narrows her eyes. "I wish we'd never been friends."

My stomach sinks, and I clench my fists until my wrists ache. All I can do is watch her back as she leaves the gym with her moms.

Later, after Pipo and Fautina have faded away to wherever they go when the power of my diary wears out, I say goodbye to Juan Carlos and trudge up the sidewalk to my house. I spot Abuelito on the porch, puffing on a cigar and blowing smoke into the evening air. I plop down on the steps next to him, needing to catch my breath.

"¿Cómo andas, mi vida?" Abuelito asks. "¿Cómo te fue la fiesta? ¿Y el novio?"

"I wasn't at a party. And I don't have a boyfriend." I pull

my glasses off and clean the lenses on the bottom of my shirt. The left lens pops out and clatters down the porch steps. I grab it, snap it back in place, and ram the glasses back on my face.

Abuelito raises his eyebrow and grunts, smacking on his cigar.

"I was watching Keisha's fencing tournament with Juan Carlos. But it didn't end well. She lost in pretty much the most unfair way possible. And . . . she got mad at me."

I sigh and lean my head against Abuelito's leg. We listen to the crickets echo in the neighborhood as the sun lowers behind the tree line. I lift my chin to the cool breeze and watch the clouds turn from burnt orange to purple as the sun sets.

"Sabes que el cielo en Cuba es más bonito, ¿no?" Abuelito says, pointing to the horizon with his cigar.

I chuckle. "Abuelito, I'm pretty sure the sky looks the same in Port Ballí as it does in Cuba."

Abuelito shakes his head and straightens up in his folding chair. "No, mi vida. Las estrellas siempre son más bonitas en tu país."

I look at my abuelito. This is Peak Cubanity, but I just don't get it.

Papi told me once that Abuelita's parents were taken away by Castro's soldiers before she was able to escape to the United States. She never saw them again. He also said that Abuelito himself fled to the United States after he spent three years in prison for protesting against the government in favor of free elections. Of course, Abuelito and Abuelita would never tell me these things themselves.

"How can you think the stars are brighter in Cuba? How can you love a country that has done so many bad things to you?"

Abuelito pats my shoulder. "Cuba no me hizo nada. Solo Castro. Mi mamá siempre me decía que un país es más que un hombre."

I have to agree. That's true here in the United States too—that a country is more than just one man. But then I think about El Cocodrilo and how much damage just one man can do.

"Your mom told you that?" I ask. I've never heard Abuelito talk about his mom.

Abuelito takes in a sharp breath, as if suddenly realizing that thoughts about his mother have escaped his mouth.

I nudge his leg with my shoulder. "Will you tell me about her? About my great-grandmother? I'd like to know what she was like."

Abuelito purses his lips, and for a moment I'm afraid he isn't going to say anything. I pick at the zipper on my backpack and wait for him to respond.

"Bueno, mi mamá Migdalia siempre olía a las flores que crecían detrás de nuestra casa," Abuelito finally says. "Y podía coser cualquier cosa que quisiera, sin patrón."

I chuckle, digging the diary out of my bag while avoiding the pieces of the destroyed effigy I shoved inside. I write on a clean page,

My great-grandmother smelled like flowers and could sew anything without a pattern.

"She sounds like magic." Thinking I could probably use her magic, I ask Abuelito, "Anything else?"

Patting the top of my head, he chuckles. As the crickets chirp louder in the front yard, he tells me how his mother broke up fights between him and Pipo with bribes of sweet natilla. How once, when Pipo and Abuelito were arguing about who could climb a coconut tree faster, his mom scampered up to the top, beating them both.

I'm busy listing everything in my diary when I hear Abuelito's voice catch in his throat.

"Pero me fui. Nunca la volví a ver," he says. He flicks his cigar with his thumb over and over. His lips press in a tight line.

He's done talking.

"But you had to leave, Abuelito. You had to escape to be safe," I tell him. "I'm sorry you never got to see her again."

Resting my head back on his knee, I close my diary. I pick at the corner of the cover until a piece breaks off between my fingers.

I think about the way Abuelito cradles his effigy before he burns it on New Year's. I always wondered why he did that. Maybe he's thinking about his mother, his brother, and everything he left behind in Cuba.

But I hid my effigy in my hoodie because I was embarrassed. Heat rushes to my cheeks, and I sigh.

Abuelito pats me on the head. "¿Todo bien, mi vida?"

I slip my diary into my bag and stand. "Yeah, I'm fine. Thanks for telling me about your mom. You can talk about her anytime you want, you know. I like hearing about your family."

Because even though I need Abuelito's stories to help me break the curse, it's true.

I kiss Abuelito on the cheek and head inside the house. Sneaking past Papi watching a basketball game in the living room and Liset and Mami arguing in the bathroom about what color Liset is allowed to dye her hair, I finally reach my room.

I toss my backpack in the corner by my music stand. The zipper comes open on its own and the pieces of the effigy fall out. Black fabric and dusty stuffing litter the floor. I watch as one of the threads hanging from the effigy squirms and morphs into a thick black worm. It wiggles free from the doll and tries to crawl across the floor and onto my foot. I kick it away quickly and it disappears under my bed.

Before I can collect the pieces of the effigy, there's a

knock on my door. No one in my family ever knocks, and I know Keisha doesn't want to see my face.

"C'mon in, Juanito," I call.

The door opens, and Juan Carlos shuffles into my room. His eyes look tired, with dark shadows underneath, and they dart to each corner of my room. His skin is pale, and he licks his lips as he shoves his hands into the pockets of his jeans.

"You okay there? You don't look so good," I tell him.

"Oh, I'm fine," he says, stretching his neck and rolling his shoulders. "I've never felt freer."

"What are you talking about?"

Juan Carlos shrugs and bites his lip, his skin looking almost green in the low light of my bedroom. "You remember in second grade when we were supposed to bring snacks to class? Your dad made merenguitos, but you thought the class would say they were weird, so you threw them away and told our teacher you forgot to bring anything."

His voice sounds scratchy, like he hasn't had a drink in an entire week. I don't know what happened to him after I left the community center, but it can't have been good.

"Yeah," I answer cautiously. "That wasn't one of my better moments. I know I hurt Papi's feelings just because I was embarrassed about our Cubanity. But why are you bringing that up?"

Juan Carlos chews on his fingernails with more force than usual. I'm afraid he's going to rip them right off with his teeth. "And you remember when you pretended you didn't know your abuelitos last year during the Fourth of July parade when they started dancing in the street to the band music?"

I feel like I'm going to throw up. I don't know why Juan Carlos is bringing up my worst moments. "They like to dance merengue and salsa any chance they get. I know I shouldn't have done that, but Mykenzye was making a big deal about it."

Juan Carlos's eyes dart around my room again, and he hunches over, his feet shuffling on the floor.

Heat sears my cheeks, and my palms sweat. "Why are you talking about all this, Juanito?"

He stops fidgeting and looks at me. "Because you're ashamed of your family. You're embarrassed of where you're from. And that's why all this is happening."

Juan Carlos leans closer to my face as I sit on my bed. I scoot back as his eyes darken. A flash of pain erupts on my arm, a burning ache sinking into my skin.

"All this is your fault."

I swallow hard. "What?"

"If you had burned the effigy like your abuelitos wanted, none of this would have happened. But you're right, too." Juan Carlos licks his lips again and narrows his eyes. "Your family is ridiculous, and it's embarrassing to be around you. Why can't you just be like everyone else?"

Tears pool in the corners of my eyes, and I grip the blanket on my bed. Even when Mykenzye is at her worst, making fun of my family's Cubanity, Juan Carlos always defends me. I don't understand how he could change his mind. "Why . . . why are you saying all this, Juanito?"

Juan Carlos straightens up and smirks. "Just stay away from me. I don't want you or your family's weirdness rubbing off. I don't want to end up like Keisha."

He turns on his heel and walks out of my room.

Tucking my knees to my chest, I wrap my arms around my legs as tears flow down my cheeks. Keisha is furious with me; Juan Carlos has abandoned me. It's just me and my family's traditions that got me into this mess in the first place.

With Juan Carlos's words still hanging in the air, I look down at the floor and notice three thick black worms squirm across the floor and through the door, following him out of my house.

EIGHTEEN

ON SUNDAY NIGHT I dreamed of being alone on a small boat in the middle of a raging storm, like in the story Fautina told. Waves crashed into the side of the boat, filling it with water. I screamed for help until my voice was hoarse. Then, a large boat pulled up, and I saw Keisha and Juan Carlos on the bow and yelled to them for help.

But they just looked at me with black eyes and shook their heads as they floated away, swallowed by the dark waves.

When I woke up, sweat covered my back, and I had kicked all my blankets to the floor.

I'm all alone. I'm going to have to figure out how to defeat El Cocodrilo by myself.

But maybe I can still use my gift. I just need to call in reinforcements like I did with Pipo and Fautina. That way I won't have to handle everything on my own.

I'm awake way earlier than I want to be on Monday morning, but I march into the kitchen, where my abuelitos sit at the table drinking café con leche. Abuelito listens as Abuelita reads out loud from her Bible.

"Mi cielo, ¿ya te despertaste?" Abuelita asks. Her eyes roam to my messy hair, the dark circles under my eyes, and the wrinkles covering my pajamas.

I shrug. "I couldn't sleep."

Abuelito pours me a cup of café, adding more milk than coffee and three spoonfuls of sugar as I join them at the table.

Leaning over the mug, I inhale the sweet steam and close my eyes. This is definitely a tradition I've always been okay with.

I set my diary on the table and open it to a clean page. Tugging down the sleeve of my pajamas so Abuelita doesn't see the mark that still sits on my forearm, I twirl my pencil between my fingers.

"Can I ask you more questions?" I say, clearing my throat and glancing at the Bible sitting next to Abuelita's coffee mug. "Could you tell me about the people listed on the family tree?"

Abuelita takes a deep breath and runs her hand over the cover of the Bible as I sip my café con leche. For a moment, I'm afraid she'll say no, just like I thought Abuelito would on the porch last night. But that day in the backyard she was almost excited to tell Keisha, Juan Carlos, and me about Fautina. I'm hoping that'll happen again.

"¿Esto es para la escuela?" Abuelita asks, scanning the multiple scabs on my hands and my completely chewed-off fingernails as I grip the diary.

"It's not just for school," I tell her. "I'd like to know more about our relatives, if that's okay with you. I mean, you told me I should write my memories in this diary, right? It would be nice if some of my memories were about people I never got to meet in Cuba."

I take another sip of my coffee and realize I'm telling the truth. I'm not manipulating my abuelitos to tell me more about our family so these people can show up and help me. I genuinely want to know.

Abuelita slowly opens her Bible to the page with the family tree and gazes at the names. But she still doesn't say anything. I start to wonder why she gave me the diary to begin with.

"¿Por qué no, mi flor? Dales vida con nuestras memorias," Abuelito says.

I smile at him. He doesn't know just how right he is, that Abuelita will be giving them life with her memories. What I wrote about Migdalia already has small flower blooms around the paragraph. My hand waits over a blank diary page, ready to bring our other relatives into this world.

Abuelita slides the Bible toward me and points to the family tree. I see her name listed at the bottom next to Abuelito's name, a small line joining them. Next to Abuelito's name is Baldomero Feijoo, and above both their names is just one, their mom, Migdalia Feijoo.

Above Abuelita's name is Felipe and Flora Crespo, her parents, and then above Felipe are Perucho and Fautina Crespo. Ramón and Margot are written next to Felipe, and underneath them, I see Andaluz's name. Next to Flora are two people named Emilio and Rogelia. I guess that makes them Abuelita's aunt and uncle. Underneath Rogelia's name is Ladislao, making him Abuelita's cousin.

"Abuelito told me about his mom, Migdalia, last night," I say. I look at Abuelito and smile. "She sounded like an amazing person."

Abuelito's eyes twinkle, and he nods.

Scanning the family tree, I point to Ladislao. "What about him? I remember Papi said one time that was a name he and Mami picked out while she was pregnant with me. Is that from your cousin?"

A smile creeps on Abuelita's face, and she brushes a finger over Ladislao's name. "Sí. Mi primito."

Abuelita sighs and then tells me all about Ladislao, her younger cousin. I copy everything she says into my diary.

Ladislao Ramirez once decided he was going to sell rooster feathers. But instead of waiting for the rooster to lose its feathers, he held it down and plucked it. Ladislao ended up with more scratches from the rooster than he did money from the neighbors.

I laugh as I read over what I wrote. I think Ladislao and Juan Carlos would've been good friends.

But thinking about Juan Carlos make my stomach churn all over again, and I take another big sip of café con leche to calm it down.

"What happened to Ladislao? Did he come to the United States?" I ask.

Abuelita closes the Bible as I tap my pencil on the diary page. After a few taps, my pencil sticks to the words I wrote. The entire page has a shiny reflection, as if someone covered it in tacky, clear paint. It's kind of gross.

Abuelita slowly shakes her head, and her shoulders sag. "No, mi cielo. Se enfermó y se murió. Una tragedia para mis tíos."

I try to add what Abuelita said to my paragraph but as I write

He got sick and died

my pencil sticks to the page. When I lift the tip, a string of goo trails from the end to the paper.

Abuelito looks curiously at my diary, and I slam it shut, leaving the pencil inside.

Abuelita gets up from the table and turns to the kitchen sink, busying herself with washing a plate that's already clean. She's done talking about family. She's done remembering the past.

Mami and Papi come down the hallway, and I slide the diary onto my lap.

"Buenos días, familia Feijoo," Papi says as he enters the kitchen. He's always unreasonably enthusiastic in the morning. When he sees me, his eyebrows raise. I still look like I put myself through the washing machine on the heavy setting.

"You okay there, kiddo? Why are you up so early?" he asks, pouring himself a cup of coffee.

I pull my mug closer to me, more than a little annoyed with my parents for interrupting my interview with my abuelitos but hoping I have enough anyway. "I wanted a chance at the coffee before you drank it all," I tell him, winking.

Papi's laugh echoes through the kitchen as Mami reaches around him and pours herself a cup.

"Too loud," she mumbles.

Mami is the opposite of Papi in the morning.

Holding her mug close to her face as if she's saying a prayer, Mami looks at me. "Mari, isn't your mariachi audition this week? Is that why you're up? Are you nervous?"

All my breath leaves my lungs.

I forgot.

With everything going on with El Cocodrilo. With

Keisha being mad at me. With Juan Carlos abandoning me. I completely forgot about my audition.

My hands grip the diary in my lap. Mami and Papi sit down at the table and look at me expectantly.

"Um . . . yeah. It's on Friday," I tell them. "I guess I'm a little nervous."

I'm nervous that El Cocodrilo will make my violin burst into flames in the middle of my performance. That he'll send an army of spiders and cockroaches to crawl all over me as I play.

But I can't tell my family about any of that.

Abuelito pats me on the back and smiles. "Bueno, solo tienes que pensar que eres la última Coca-Cola en el desierto. Y ya."

Even though I might throw up the café con leche, I laugh. "Wait, what does being the last Coke in the desert have to do with anything?"

Papi chuckles. "Abuelito is just telling you to go in there and be as amazing as we know you are."

I chew on my lip. If only they knew what I was up against.

As if reminding me, the sunlight coming through the sliding door dims as a swarm of flies cover the glass. The bulb in the fixture above the kitchen table flickers, and bits of white plaster fall onto the table. I look up as thick brown cockroaches crawl out of the light and across the ceiling. I squeeze my eyes shut, knowing this is just another trick of El Cocodrilo that only I can see.

Abuelita's shrieks pierce the kitchen, and my eyes fly open.

The spiny cockroaches drop one by one from the light fixture, and everyone screams. Mami takes off her house slipper and swats at them. I brush skittering insects off the table and onto the floor with my diary. Papi grabs a broom as Abuelito pushes the rest of the cockroaches off the table with his newspaper. Papi sweeps them across the floor, and Abuelita opens the back door.

After the last fat brown bug is flung outside with Papi's broom, Mami falls into a chair at the table. "What on earth was that?" she gasps.

I shake my head and run to my room as Papi and Abuelito inspect the light above the table. The pieces of the destroyed effigy still sit next to my backpack, shriveled and black.

I poke a shaking finger at the remnants of the doll, but when I touch the fabric, a chill surges through my body and a deep voice swirls in my room.

Oh, Mari. I told you I don't need it anymore. I'm so much bigger now.

NINETEEN

PORT BALLÍ PRIMARY School has faced hurricanes and floods, experiments gone awry in the science labs, kindergarten bathrooms that required hazmat suits to enter, and cafeteria disasters condemned by the health department.

But nothing prepared any of the students or teachers for what it faced after El Cocodrilo was freed from the confines of the effigy. On Monday, Ms. Faruqi opened the laptop cart so we could all work on our world's fair projects, only to find that the cords had turned into squirming black snakes. They burst from the cart and slithered across the floor, wrapping around the feet of any student who didn't hop up on their chair.

I started to ask Juan Carlos if he was okay, but I was too afraid. He'd probably have more mean things to say to me. Ms. Faruqi immediately called the Port Ballí Wildlife Center, informing them that one of their exhibits had gotten loose.

On Tuesday, moths infested the books in the library, drowning any student in a cloud of suffocating insects. Thick maggots burst from the food in the cafeteria on Wednesday, and spiky beetles crawled from the air-conditioning vents in every classroom on Thursday. I walked down the hall each day wondering if any of the students knew this was all my fault. I wanted to get on the school intercom and scream, "I'm sorry! I'm trying to fix it!"

First thing Friday morning, slimy slugs squirmed out of the toilets in the bathrooms. It didn't take long until every single student in school walked warily down the hallways, their eyes full of fear and their arms clenched around each other for safety.

Mr. Nguyen declared that Mercury was in retrograde, but I knew the truth.

El Cocodrilo was no longer bound by the curse he'd put on me and Keisha. He could make anyone miserable if he wanted to. But even with the strangest week Port Ballí Primary School has ever seen, I still have my mariachi audition. I still have to be ready to face him when he inevitably shows up.

After classes end, I clutch my violin case to my chest and head to the music room. As I walk down the hallway, I slip on the tile and stumble. I look at the bottom of my shoe as greenish-yellow slime drips from it.

"Oh, what now?" I say, rubbing my soles on the floor.

A giggle and stomping feet echo in the hallway. A little boy runs and slides to a stop, inches from my feet. He looks at me and sticks a finger knuckle-deep in his nose.

"First-grade hallway is that way," I say, pointing to the left. His brown hair sticks out in every direction, like he hasn't brushed it for a week, and the plain gray shorts and white shirt he's wearing have more wrinkles than Ms. Faruqi.

"What's that?" he says. He takes his finger out of his nose and sneezes without covering his mouth.

"Gross, kid. You should go home. Most everybody's run screaming from the building, in case you haven't noticed."

"I can't," he replies, dragging his foot along the floor and leaving a trail of shiny slime.

I groan. "Why not?"

The boy wipes his nose with the back of his hand and then rubs his hand on the leg of his tan shorts, leaving a thick streak.

"Because you made me come here."

I look the boy up and down. "Ladislao?"

He nods and sneezes again. "So are we going to play now?"

"No. I have an audition." I chew on my lip. I hadn't realized that Ladislao was so young when he died. "I'm sorry. I think it was a mistake calling you. I'm not sure how you could help."

I pick at the hem of my hoodie, and the seam unravels, a

dark green thread hanging loose. I start to wind the thread around my finger, but it quivers and pulls away, moving back and forth and sewing itself into the fabric.

"What the frijoles?"

"That's much better," a soft voice says behind me. I spin and face a woman who's dressed in a light green dress with pink flowers embroidered along the edge. Her white hair is cut short and curled under her ears.

"Oh, thank god. You're here," I say. "I need your help."

"Wow. Who's she?" Ladislao asks, jumping up and down and clapping.

"I'm pretty sure this is my abuelito's mom, Migdalia," I tell him.

Migdalia nods and snaps her fingers. "My sweet, let's be quick. Because you're in a mess."

"I know. My abuelo said you were the best seamstress in Cuba. I think I need you to make something for me."

Migdalia purses her lips. Ladislao moves closer to her. She examines him and holds up her hand, taking a step away. Turning back to me, she says, "I assume you have a plan."

I chew on the inside of my mouth. "It's more the beginning of a plan that I hope will work. Someone told me the dead are connected to objects. That the more precious the item is, the better. Do you think it's possible to call on someone if the object is important to the caller and not so much to the person you're trying to call on?"

Migdalia tucks a strand of hair behind her ear and smiles softly. "I believe it's possible. I used to call on my ancestors by embroidering their names on handkerchiefs."

"I did it by sneezing," Ladislao pipes up.

I look at him and raise an eyebrow. "No, you did not."

He nods furiously. "Yes, I did. I'd think of them and let out a big sneeze. The more snot, the better."

I can't believe I was almost named after this booger ball.

Migdalia rolls her eyes. "Anyway, what are you thinking, my dear?"

I set my violin case down, not daring to hand it to Ladislao, and unzip my Houston Aeros hoodie. "This is my favorite hoodie ever. My abuelitos saved up for months to buy it for me because they know I love hockey. I want you to make an effigy out of this."

Migdalia smiles. I wait for her to take the hoodie, but I realize it would just fall through her fingers. She waves her hand, and the hoodie shakes, the fabric quivering as threads come loose and dance in the air. I let go of the hoodie, and it stays suspended, morphing and changing as the sleeves tuck into the body, the bottom edge is sewn closed, and the hood becomes a stuffed head.

Placing her hands on her hips, Migdalia winks as the new effigy floats into my hands. "Not my best work, but it will do. Now, what on earth are we going to do with that?"

I take a deep breath. "El Cocodrilo is definitely going to

show up at my audition. There's no way he can resist messing it up. So I want to try to catch him. His weakness has to be something to do with effigies. Even though he destroyed my old doll, that one didn't really mean anything to me—it was just one of Papi's shirts. But this one definitely does."

I run my hand over the dark green fabric. The airplane emblem sits on the stomach of the new effigy like a shield.

"Do you think we could trap him in this?" I ask, looking from Migdalia to Ladislao. "My friend Juan Carlos said that since effigies absorb despair and El Cocodrilo is basically made up of sadness, maybe he could actually be sucked into the doll."

"Trapped in a doll?" Ladislao groans. "That sounds horrible!"

Migdalia tilts her head. "It certainly wouldn't hurt to try."

I pick up my violin case and sling it over my shoulder. "Okay. So I'll draw in El Cocodrilo with my audition and let's see if the two of you can use the effigy to trap him. Like maybe undo the seams and see if it'll suck him in?"

"You've listened to too many scary stories," Ladislao huffs.

I shrug. He's not wrong.

We head down the hall toward the music room as my palms sweat and my stomach flip-flops.

When we reach the door, Ladislao fidgets next to me. "We get to play with this crocodile guy now?" he asks.

I smirk. "Yes."

TWENTY

I MARCH INTO the music room, Migdalia and Ladislao following me. In the chaos of the students tuning their instruments, adjusting music stands, and rummaging through sheet music, no one notices that I'm accompanied by a grandma and a snotty kid. Besides, Manuel Reyes is too busy trying to figure out why the felt that lines the inside of his guitarrón case has turned into cactus spines, and Carla Mendez keeps blowing fat, pulsing worms out of her trumpet every time she plays it.

El Cocodrilo's mischief has seeped into the music room.

I motion for Migdalia and Ladislao to hide, pointing to a rack of costumes from the fourth grade's Texas history play.

"Wait for El Cocodrilo to show up, and then we'll try to trap him in this," I tell them, placing the new effigy at their feet as they hide behind pioneer dresses and long military coats.

Ladislao brushes a hand against the sleeve of a coat, his

fingers dipping into the fabric, and leaves a streak of slime dripping from the cloth. "We'll get him. You just play your violin."

Migdalia gives me a reassuring smile and I head to my usual seat next to Ines.

"Nervous?" Ines asks, her leg bouncing up and down as she puts her chin pad on her violin. "After the day we just had," she says, "I'm hoping I even remember how to read music. This is the third chin pad I've used. The first two squirmed like slugs right off my instrument!"

I nod, unsure what to say. "I'm a little nervous, I guess. But we'll do the best we can, right?"

Ines winks and fine-tunes her strings. "Exactly. And I know you'll do fine. I really like the way you play."

I can't help but smile. "Thanks. Honestly, I don't want to audition after you. You're going to be amazing. I think I'd rather go after Marco," I say and laugh, pointing to a boy trying to pick his nose with the tip of his bow. He'd probably be good friends with Ladislao.

Glancing behind me, I spot Ladislao peeking from between two dresses, a bubble of snot growing out of his nostril. But past him, a trail of ants march along the wall, heading toward me.

My heartbeat thuds in my ears, but Ines nudges me with her elbow.

"That's the first time I've heard you laugh in a while.

Is everything okay? Well, aside from all the weird things happening at school."

I sigh, my shoulders sagging. I chew on the inside of my mouth, almost drawing blood in my frustration. "You know, when you get a mosquito bite, it's annoying and itchy, but at least it's just one bite?"

Ines raises her eyebrows. "Yeah, I guess."

The ants pool at Ladislao's feet, and he lets out a silent but powerful sneeze, covering them in snot. They freeze on the carpet.

"Let's just say I've been getting at least five mosquito bites a day for the past couple of weeks," I tell Ines. "All put together, I just want to curl up into a ball and not exist anymore."

"You're talking about Mykenzye, aren't you?" Ines asks.

As if summoned like a demon from the muddiest gulf waters, Mykenzye walks into the music room. She strides up to us, a notebook in her hand, swatting at her hair as four mosquitoes fly from the strands.

"What are you doing here?" I ask, trying to keep my voice from shaking. The last thing I need is for her to spot my ghost relatives hiding in the corner, El Cocodrilo in all his rabid insect glory, or me completely messing up my audition.

Mykenzye shrugs, smoothing her hair with her hand as one final mosquito creeps from behind her ear. "I'm covering the Mexican music for Spanish Heritage Month or whatever. Aren't you guys supposed to be wearing big hats?"

Ines rolls her eyes. "It's mariachi music. And Hispanic and Latinx Heritage Month is in September. Not January."

Mykenzye doesn't answer, turning from us with a flip of her hair and sitting next to Mr. Quintera.

"That's exactly what I'm talking about," Ines whispers to me. "I was in the same class with her last year, and she did the same thing to me. Little comments and questions that shouldn't be a big deal by themselves, but all put together, they make your life miserable. My mom told me they were microaggressions. It isn't like Mykenzye stands on her chair in the middle of class shouting 'I hate Latinx people,' but what she does is just as ignorant and hurtful."

I take a deep breath and swallow hard. I've never heard Mykenzye's actions explained like that. And I can't help but think that she and El Cocodrilo would get along well.

Before I can ask Ines what she did about Mykenzye's microaggressions, Mr. Quintera calls us all to attention and tells us to shake off our nerves from the unbelievably strange day we've all had.

I glance behind me to make sure Migdalia and Ladislao are well hidden. Then I scan the room for any sign of bugs.

So far, no Cocodrilo.

Mr. Quintera clears his throat and begins the auditions with the trumpets and guitars. Then he moves on to the guitarrones and violas. All I can think about as they play is how much I don't want to audition in front of Mykenzye. I should just run out of the room. Tell Mr. Quintera I got sick and ask to audition some other time.

But I've got to make this stop. I've got to catch El Cocodrilo, even if Mykenzye watches me do it.

When the last viola plays, the lighting in the room slightly darkens. I turn around as a thick layer of flies and moths dot the windows. My heartbeat quickens, and I gesture at Migdalia to be ready. She gives me a sharp nod.

"And now for our final group—the violins," Mr. Quintera says, tapping his clipboard with his fingers. "Let's begin with Ines."

I pat Ines on the back and wish her luck. I'm certain she'll do better than I will.

She plays a perfect rendition of "México Lindo y Querido" and then plays her own piece, "Cielito Lindo." I smile as she plays, her clear bow strokes and strong notes filling the room. She's amazing. Even poor Mr. Quintera wipes a tear from his eye when she's done.

When Ines sits back down, Mr. Quintera calls, "Maricela Feijoo."

"Of course," I mutter.

"Good luck," Ines whispers, giving me a wink.

I walk to the front of the room, my violin tucked under my arm, and set my sheet music on the stand. It promptly falls over with a loud clatter.

"Here we go," I mumble under my breath as the mark

on my arm burns. Migdalia and Ladislao are still hiding behind the row of costumes, their gazes fixed on the windows. The flies and moths have increased and are joined by large wasps. Migdalia creeps out from behind a clump of dresses, her fists clenched.

"Ready, Mari?" Mr. Quintera asks, his pen hovering over his clipboard. Everyone stares at me at the front of the music room, oblivious to the battle that's about to go down behind them. Mykenzye slides her phone out of her pocket and points the camera at me. My shirt sticks to my back with sweat.

"I guess so," I reply, and then correct myself. "Yes, sir."

I take a deep breath and raise my bow to begin my piece. I look at my sheet music, but the notes have swirled, freeing themselves from the treble clef. They stretch and squirm, turning into long worms crawling over the page. I take another deep breath, determined to play "México Lindo y Querido." I lower my bow to the strings and begin playing, a moment of relief washing over me as the notes come out clear, filling the room. I continue playing and let myself sway to the music. I watch Mr. Quintera tap his foot along to the song as Mykenzye records me.

That's when I see him.

Seated on the windowsill, behind the class and out of sight, El Cocodrilo snarls, his teeth bared. His eyes narrow and fix on my violin. He slowly shakes his head as his lips curl and his tongue darts in and out of his mouth.

I continue playing, but my stomach flutters. Migdalia waves her fingers, and the effigy floats in front of her. Ladislao creeps out from behind a long coat and flings his hand at the wall beneath El Cocodrilo, where a line of spiders skitter down to the floor. They're paralyzed by a layer of slime.

As I play my song, El Cocodrilo flicks his finger once, twice, three times and then at my bow as three hairs snap one after the other. I keep playing as the broken hairs hang loose from the top of my bow. El Cocodrilo continues flicking his fingers, his black eyes narrowed. I watch helplessly as I play, but more and more hairs on my bow snap until they all drape from the tip, useless.

I lower my violin in the middle of the song and hold out the bow to Mr. Quintera, showing him the broken, hanging hairs.

Ines runs up to me and hands me her bow. "Here. Use mine. You were doing great."

"Class, this is a good lesson in why we shouldn't overtighten our bows," Mr. Quintera announces.

Mykenzye smirks and holds her phone up higher. "For the newspaper," she tells Mr. Quintera.

I want to roll my eyes, but I stop myself. Migdalia inches closer to El Cocodrilo, the effigy floating behind her as she waves her fingers. One seam along the head of the doll is open, the threads reaching out toward El Cocodrilo, grasping toward his toes as they dangle from the windowsill.

I stare at El Cocodrilo, trying to keep his attention so he doesn't notice Migdalia approaching or Ladislao, who continues to cover the insects and arachnids trying to reach me with slime. I examine El Cocodrilo's face, the heavy, dark bags hanging below his black eyes. His chest heaves, struggling to draw breath, as his hands tremble under his scaly skin.

I almost feel sorry for him.

And then three strings on my violin snap with an off-key twang, and he smiles, his yellow teeth dripping with saliva.

"Mari, is everything all right?" Mr. Quintera asks.

"No . . . not really," I stammer. I look pleadingly at Ines, who runs up with her own violin and hands it to me.

"I'm not sure what's happening, but keep going. You can do it," she whispers.

I pluck the strings on Ines's violin before raising it to my chin. Even with El Cocodrilo sabotaging everything and Mykenzye recording it all, I have to keep going. I have to make this stop.

"Why don't you continue with the piece you prepared?" Mr. Quintera suggests, setting his clipboard on the chair next to him.

I straighten my shoulders and steady myself. I had originally practiced "Las Mañanitas," but I change my mind. If this audition is going to be a disaster, it might as well be the most Cuban disaster ever.

My abuelitos would appreciate that.

I lift my bow and draw out the opening notes of "Guantanamera." El Cocodrilo's chest shudders as he takes a deep breath. His black eyes lighten to golden irises, and the hard line of his mouth softens as he listens to Cuba's unofficial national anthem, the lyrics based on a poem by José Martí, Cuba's unofficial patron saint.

Basically, my audition piece is Peak Cubanity.

As I play, I think of my abuelitos, surviving so much to start over in a new country. I close my eyes as I think of Pipo, Fautina, Migdalia, Ladislao, and even Andaluz—relatives I didn't know I had who've come to help me. I let the notes wash over me and I sway to the music.

Opening my eyes, I catch El Cocodrilo tapping along to the song, his hand on his thigh. His mouth settles into a slight smile as his foot sways back and forth to my playing. His skin glistens as the scales seem to fade, replaced by suntanned skin.

I focus on my song as Migdalia approaches even closer, now hovering the effigy directly below El Cocodrilo's foot. I struggle to remember the right notes as I watch El Cocodrilo's toes stretch toward the effigy, as if they're being sucked in by the threads reaching out to him like slithering snakes.

This is it. We've got him. He's going to get trapped in the effigy, where he won't be able to harass Keisha, me, or anyone else again.

I continue my song with new strength, and a smile creeps along my face.

But then El Cocodrilo's eyes dart down and catch Migdalia. The gray scales burst from his skin again. He snaps his fingers, and the new effigy falls apart along the seams, piece by piece. He sneers at Ladislao, and then his black eyes meet mine. He jerks his head from side to side and snarls. The note I'm playing falls flat and growls. I keep moving my bow, adjusting my fingers to try to fix the note, but the sound grows louder and becomes a high-pitched scream that makes everyone in the class cover their ears and squeeze their eyes shut.

That's when six wasps squeeze themselves out of the inside of the violin and swarm toward my face. I drop Ines's violin and flail my arms to get the wasps away from me.

"I think that's enough," Mr. Quintera says, shaking his head.

Mykenzye lowers her phone and says, "I'm so posting this."

I watch as Midgalia backs away, her form slowly fading as she presses Ladislao behind her, protecting him from El Cocodrilo's snarls. Eventually, they disappear, and all I see is El Cocodrilo's smile before he vanishes in a cloud of black flies that swirl and sail out the window.

TWENTY-ONE

MY FINGERS HOVER over my cell phone. I want to text Keisha and Juan Carlos and tell them about my audition. About what El Cocodrilo did, and how Migdalia and Ladislao tried to help. About Mykenzye showing up and what Ines said.

But they don't want to talk to me.

I have no one. Except the ghost family members I manage to conjure up.

Sitting on the front steps of my house, I push aside the torn pieces of my Houston Aeros hoodie and pull the diary out of my backpack. I open it to Fautina's page, which is covered with drawings. She has to know the most about El Cocodrilo and how we can trap him. He was her father, after all.

I find a broken pencil in the bottom of my bag and start writing.

Fautina was my abuelita's abuelita. She had bright red

fingernails and silvery hair. When she told stories, they came alive in front of everyone, like beautiful butterflies flying through the air. Her voice was soft like a lullaby and her eyes would sparkle when she talked.

At least that's how I remember her.

I watch as my words swirl on the page, blossoming into crimson flower petals floating across a glistening starry sky. I hope that's a sign Fautina is on her way.

Shoving the diary into my backpack, I trudge into my house. The living room and kitchen are empty. Mami and Papi are still at school, and Liset is at powerlifting practice.

I continue through to the backyard and see my abuelitos sitting at the patio table. Abuelita is hemming the leg on a pair of Abuelito's pants, her needle and thread weaving through the fabric with ease.

"¡Oye, mi vida! ¿Cómo te fue la audición?" Abuelito asks, smacking his hands together.

I open my mouth to tell him, but all that comes out are choked sobs as tears stream down my face. It was obvious my audition was going to be a disaster, but it still hurt. I tried to follow Pipo's advice and not react to all the trouble El Cocodrilo causes, to all the ways he's twisting my world. But I've swallowed so much, it's grown and grown in my belly. Now, like an overfilled balloon, I think I might burst.

I sit down next to Abuelita and put my head in her lap.

"Ay, mi cielo. Está bien. A veces lo único que puedes

hacer es llorar," Abuelita says, setting her sewing project on the table and rubbing my back.

Since Abuelita says that sometimes the only thing you can do is cry, I do. I close my eyes and let tears soak through the apron tied around Abuelita's waist. Tears for Keisha and Juan Carlos—tears for every little crack that El Cocodrilo put in my way—drown the small white flowers on Abuelita's apron fabric.

She runs her fingers through my hair as we sit in the backyard, the cool breeze swirling through the mango trees. Abuelito hums a song, and I breathe deep as the tune warms my heart.

I listen closely to Abuelito's song as a violin joins his melody. I open my eyes and see an image of myself standing in the backyard, my instrument under my chin. I'm five years younger and surrounded by my family as I play my first song. Wiping tears from my cheeks, I watch as my parents clap along with my song as Liset sticks her fingers in her ears. When Younger Me finishes her song, she takes a dramatic bow while my abuelitos and parents cheer enthusiastically, their cries tumbling over the grass and tickling my ears.

I sit up and look at my abuelitos. Could they see the same scene in the backyard that I did? Abuelito rubs his eyes as Abuelita shakes her head.

They definitely saw.

"I can explain," I tell them, brushing my hair out of my face.

But before I can, Fautina walks around from the side of the house and into the backyard. Her purple skirt and silver hair stay still despite the gulf breeze blowing through our yard.

Abuelita yelps and launches her chancla at Fautina. It passes directly through her and tumbles across the grass, making Abuelita scream even louder.

Abuelito starts to stand, but I grab his arm. "Wait. I can explain. Just don't freak out."

Telling a Cuban not to freak out is like telling a jellyfish not to sting.

"This is Fautina Crespo. Your abuela," I tell Abuelita.

She looks Fautina up and down and takes her in with curious eyes. She covers her mouth with a shaking hand and whispers, "No puede ser."

"Yes, it's true. She showed up after I wrote about her in the diary you gave me for New Year's."

"Pero eso fue solo un libro. Un regalo normal . . ." Abuelita stammers.

Fautina climbs our patio steps and sits down in a chair as I realize that she's not the only thing I have to explain to my abuelitos.

"It wasn't just a regular gift. Trust me." I take a deep breath. "Turns out I have a special ability, something a lot of people in our family could do. We thought we lost it when we left Cuba, but apparently, I have it."

I hold the diary in my hands, trying to keep them from shaking as I talk. "I can make our dead relatives appear by writing about them in this book. Abuelito, I wrote about your brother Pipo, and I got to meet him. He's amazing. And I met your mom, too, and she's incredible."

Abuelito looks at me with wide eyes and rubs his fingers over his chin, thinking. Abuelita smooths her hands on her apron and stares at Fautina. Abuelito chuckles, the deep sound startling me. He takes the notebook from me and flips to Pipo's page. "¿Los cuentos eran ciertos? ¿De verdad?"

Abuelita turns her wide eyes to Abuelito and shakes her head. "Mis padres y mis abuelos siempre hablaban de nuestra magia, pero nunca les creía."

"Wait," I say, taking in what my abuelitos said. "You knew about the gift?"

Fautina clears her throat. "They thought it was simply stories or memories that became distorted and unbelievable over time. Tales passed down by old folks given to superstition."

I wrap my hand around Abuelito's. I can feel the calluses on his fingers from his working in his garden every day. I trace my thumb over the scars on his wrists from his time in Cuba, their origins unspoken.

"It's true," I say. "It's not just a story. It may have skipped a generation, but it's here, with me." I take a deep breath. The realization that I carry so much more of Cuba in me than my abuelitos ever imagined forms a lump in my throat.

Abuelito squeezes my hand. "Nunca debimos haberte ocultado nuestras historias. Habrías encontrado tu poder antes."

I shake my head. "I understand why you didn't want to tell me stories about Cuba. It's painful to talk about things you lost. And I don't think I could've handled finding out about my power any sooner—because I can barely handle it now!"

Abuelita pats me on the leg and smiles, her eyes beaming with pride.

Fautina speaks up. "Mari, don't you think we should tell your abuelitos about the more pressing matter?"

I deflate. Taking off my glasses, I clean them on the edge of my shirt, careful to avoid all the taped parts. "Okay, since you seem to be cool with the fact that Fautina is here and you have a granddaughter who can make ghosts appear," I say, straightening in my chair, "this won't seem too strange, but there's been something going on."

I launch into the saga of the effigy on New Year's Eve and El Cocodrilo cursing me and Keisha with bad luck. Fautina's fingers dance in the air as the grass in our backyard swirls and flattens into the tile at Port Ballí Primary

School. My abuelitos watch as spiders skitter down hallways, cafeteria lunches come alive, and violin strings swirl.

A smile breaks out on Abuelito's face when Pipo appears, and I tell them how he scared El Cocodrilo away. Abuelita covers her mouth in horror as I describe El Cocodrilo threatening us in the hallway and then his scaly, hunched-over form appears in the backyard.

When I finish telling the story, the mango trees reappear as the school music room and my failed audition fade away.

I look tentatively from Abuelito to Abuelita. I bite my nails and glance at Fautina, waiting for anyone to speak.

Abuelito takes a deep breath. "Bueno, eso le zumba el mango." He reaches into the chest pocket of his guayabera and takes out a cigar. Rolling it between his fingers, he glances at Abuelita.

"But it's not unbelievable. It's true!" I say. I push up the sleeve of my shirt and show them the mark on my arm.

Abuelita grabs me and examines my skin closely. She starts to get up, and I know she's planning on slathering me with Vivaporu.

"Don't bother, Abuelita. It won't come off. Trust me."

Abuelita slaps her hands on her lap. "Entonces, ¿cómo le damos un chancletazo a ese mocoso?"

I chuckle. "I don't think hitting El Cocodrilo with

a sandal will work. We need a better plan. And I think I know a way," I say, twisting my hands in my lap. "I tried something with Migdalia."

"Mi mamá?" Abuelito asks, his eyes lighting up.

I nod as Abuelito smiles. "Yep. I wrote about how you told me she was this amazing seamstress, and she showed up right before my mariachi audition."

Abuelito chuckles and slaps his leg.

"Abuelita's cousin Ladislao showed up, too, and he's kinda gross, but not totally useless. We tried trapping El Cocodrilo in a new effigy, and it almost worked. His foot got sucked into it, but then he destroyed the effigy, and the effect stopped."

Fautina clicks her tongue. "That's incredible. How were you able to do that?"

I chew on the inside of my mouth and adjust my glasses, trying to describe the idea that's taking shape in my head. "I was playing 'Guantanamera' for my audition, and his skin started to change and look more human. I think the song brought back memories from his old life and made him weaker. Do you think if we tried something like that again, with maybe a new effigy and more people, it might actually work next time?"

Abuelita and Abuelito look at each other as Fautina smooths her hands on her skirt.

"It would help to have as many relatives as possible, no?" Fautina says. "Pipo, Migdalia, and Ladislao. Is there anyone else?"

I rub the back of my neck. "There's one more person I called. Andaluz. She scared the caca out of me in the school bathroom, and I've been too afraid to call on her again. But maybe she could help. She was able to fight El Cocodrilo off before."

Abuelita takes in a sharp breath at the mention of her cousin, and she nods.

Tugging on the edge of my shirt, I sigh. "I need to make things right with Keisha and Juan Carlos too. Keisha should be here, since she's cursed too, and it was Juan Carlos's idea to trap El Cocodrilo in the effigy in the first place."

I bounce my leg up and down, excited to finally have a solution to the mess of the past weeks.

"My dear, don't forget," Fautina says, smoothing her hands on her skirt. "There are others who could give us the support we need to fight El Cocodrilo. Others who should know what's been happening to you this entire time."

I tilt my head to the side. "Who?"

"Your parents."

My stomach sinks to the soles of my shoes. "Oh."

TWENTY-TWO

ON MONDAY MORNING, I sit at the kitchen table scribbling in my diary, copying the pages Abuelito wrote out last night about his brother. I convinced them to wait on telling Mami and Papi about this whole mess until I came up with a plan.

"¿Lista para mis memorias de Andaluz?" Abuelita asks, nudging me with her elbow as she drinks her café con leche. She takes a sip, purses her lips, as if the coffee tastes rancid, and pushes the cup away from her across the table.

I flip to a blank page in my diary and write

Andaluz

at the top. "Ready," I say.

As Abuelita talks, she lifts her chin and closes her eyes, as if searching in her brain for memories of her cousin, lost so long ago. I write down everything she says.

Andaluz was the best dancer in Abuelita's entire neighborhood. Abuelita loved to watch her dance to music every

Nochebuena. Andaluz told everyone she wanted to be a ballet dancer when she grew up. She wanted to perform in all the biggest cities in the world.

I read over what I have written about Andaluz and add two sentences of my own.

I wish she could've had the chance. I wish she could've found freedom.

Once I finish recording Abuelita's memories, I shove the diary into Por Si Las Moscas, hike my backpack on my shoulder, and race out the door to school. Running down the sidewalk, I pass the block in front of Dulcita Paleta Shop, and the uneven pavement makes me trip. I slam to the ground.

My elbows and knees sting, but I brush myself off and keep running, ignoring the people staring at me as they cast their fishing lines into the gulf waves. I'm nervous about having to talk to Keisha and Juan Carlos, even though I'm excited about the plan.

I just hope they'll listen to me.

I run another block and watch as the pavement in front of Ballí T-Shirt Emporium pops up, catches on my shoes, and tumbles me to the ground.

Catching my breath as I lie on the sidewalk, I push myself up again. "Oh, no you don't, you worthless watered-down walrus. Not this morning."

A large brown cormorant flies overhead and lets out

a stream of white poop that lands in my hair. I look up to the sky and shout, "Nice try, you . . . Oh, I'm on X. I got nothing."

At least I have a travel-size shampoo in Por Si Las Moscas.

When I finally make it to school, I quickly wash the bird stink bomb out of my hair and look for Keisha and Juan Carlos among the kids who are shouting about thick spiderwebs lining the inside of their lockers and fat grasshoppers bouncing from head to head in the kindergarten classrooms.

I spot Juan Carlos shoving an oversize rain poncho into Señor Listopatodo and run up to him.

"Hey, Juanito. Um . . . I know you may still be mad at me, but I've got some news," I say, unsure of how he's going to react. We haven't talked since the day of Keisha's fencing tournament.

"So you're speaking to me now?" Juan Carlos says, raising an eyebrow as he zips his backpack. A loose grasshopper skitters across the floor toward his foot, and he kicks it away.

I put my hands on my hips. "What do you mean? You're the one who wasn't speaking to me! After you showed up at my house and called me an embarrassment."

Juan Carlos's mouth drops open. "I did what?"

"You said everything that was happening was my fault

and you didn't want to be around me anymore. So I left you alone."

Juan Carlos shakes his head. "Mari, that wasn't me. I'd never say those things to you. We're Super Ojos forever, right? I'm pretty sure that was El Cocodrilo."

A chill grips my spine as the mark on my arm tingles.

"I figured you were mad at me for some reason," he says, "so I gave you space since you kept avoiding me. That's why I haven't talked to you. I wasn't going to push you."

I sigh. "Oh, thank god. Well, I've got big news."

My stomach flip-flops and my pulse races as I tell Juan Carlos about how I tried to trap El Cocodrilo with Migdalia and Ladislao, Fautina showing up again, and our plan to make the bad luck go away for good. My voice echoes off the tile floor, rising over the noisy second graders as I tell him that we need to get everyone together, alive and dead, for one last showdown with El Cocodrilo.

"Ugh. Why are you people so loud?" I hear a sneer behind me, and I turn and see Mykenzye, a smirk plastered on her face. A long line of fire-ant bites splatter across her calf, and just for a second, I'm not so mad at El Cocodrilo.

"I'm not—" I start, but another voice stops me.

"Say that again," Keisha says as she stomps across the hallway to us. "Do it. Say it again."

Mykenzye's eyes grow as big as empanadas. "What do you mean?"

Keisha shakes her head and crosses her arms. "No, what do *you* mean by 'you people'? Explain it to me."

Mykenzye shakes her head and stammers, "I . . . I was just kidding. You know how—"

"No, you weren't just kidding. Don't say stuff like that again."

Rather than argue with Keisha, which would be the stupidest decision anyone could ever make on the face of the planet, Mykenzye turns on her heel and slinks away down the hall.

I look at Keisha. "Thanks for that. I never know what to say to her."

She shrugs. "Look. I may still be mad at you and this whole mess, but no one messes with the Super Ojos. Especially not Mayonnaise Mykenzye."

I breathe a sigh of relief. "You still want to be a Super Ojo? You're not going to abandon us for Syed?"

Keisha's eyes widen. "Why would you think that? Y'all are my best friends."

I scuff my feet on the floor and kick away another grasshopper about to pounce on my shoe. "It's just that it's exactly what happened with Liset when she got her first boyfriend."

Keisha shakes her head and chuckles. "Syed isn't my boyfriend. We just like hanging out. But even if he was, I'd still never ignore you guys just because of him. And honestly, it kind of ticks me off that you think I would."

"I'm sorry." I sigh. "For everything, really. With all the curse stuff and ghost relatives on top of that, I was scared it would be too much and I'd lose you."

"I get it, and I'm sorry too. I know you didn't mean for all this curse stuff to happen." Keisha lightly punches my shoulder and smiles. "But would you be okay if Syed was a Super Ojo too? We could get him fake glasses as a joke."

Juan Carlos and I chuckle. "I think so," I tell her. "So . . . are you ready to hear about the big plan to finally fix everything?"

Keisha raises an eyebrow, and I launch into my idea, waving my arms and being as loud as I want as I talk.

Who cares if it's Peak Cubanity.

Just as I finish, the tardy bell rings and we race to Mr. Ngyuen's class. Before we can enter, our teacher stops me at the door. "Principal Gearhart asked to see you in his office," he says.

"Now? Why does he need to see me?" I ask, but Mr. Ngyuen has already herded Keisha and Juan Carlos into the classroom and shut the door.

I hurry down the hallway to the school office. My stomach flutters. I've never been called to the principal's office before. I'm definitely not a perfect student. I forget to do my homework more often than I should, and it's way too easy to yell at the squirmy first graders I always trip over, but I've never done anything to earn a visit to Principal Gearhart's office.

When I get there, the secretary isn't behind her desk. All I see is a thick snake slither down her chair and crawl behind a filing cabinet. Normal for Port Ballí these days. I don't want to waste the time I could be spending with Keisha and Juan Carlos, planning how to finally squash El Cocodrilo, so I knock on Principal Gearhart's door.

"Come in," a muffled voice says from the other side.

When I open the door, I'm hit with the smell of stale air, as if Principal Gearhart hasn't ventured outside his office for three months. Stepping into the room, a low buzzing fills my ears as flies crawl over every piece of furniture. The tall windows in front of me darken as moths, flies, and wasps cover every inch of the glass.

"It's not real, it's not real," I mumble to myself as I squeeze my eyes shut, the mark on my arm burning. "You're just here to talk to the principal."

I hear a snarl and open my eyes. The office door slams behind me, and a figure rises from the chair behind Principal Gearhart's desk, hunched over and shoulders heaving.

A scream rolls from my throat slowly, sliding across the carpeted floor, spilling against the windows, and wrapping around El Cocodrilo as he smirks. He runs one long fingernail across the desk, leaving a jagged mark in the wood.

I back against the door, trying to turn the doorknob, but it's cemented in place. The muscles in my arm spasm under the mark as it erupts in pain.

"Oh, Mari. You think I've just been playing little tricks, don't you?" El Cocodrilo snarls. He leans forward, his knuckles cracking on the desk under his weight.

My tongue sticks to the roof of my mouth as my knees shake.

"You can laugh with your little friends all you want. You can stuff those stupid satchels with anything your heart desires. You can call on whoever in our family, any of those foolish people. It won't matter."

El Cocodrilo's eyes flash bright green as he launches himself onto Principal Gearhart's desk and towers over me. Fiery ants, black cockroaches, and slithering worms pour from the sleeves of his ragged shirt and the legs of his pants, scurrying across the scratched wood.

"I know my insipid little daughter told you all about me—how I was when I was alive, what happened to me. How did it feel looking in a mirror?"

El Cocodrilo jumps forward from the desk, his black cloak flying out and stirring up the flies that have settled on the desktop.

My knees give out, and I crumple to the floor, my back pressed to the door so hard, my spine aches. I swallow hard and manage to croak out, "What are you talking about? I'm nothing like you."

El Cocodrilo crouches in front of me, inches from my face.

"Are you sure? You're ashamed of who you are. I know how you've treated your family, how you've hidden who you truly are from others."

He lifts a finger as a black fly emerges from his hairline and crawls across his forehead. He snaps his finger, and the insects covering the windows and furniture swarm as one thick cloak toward me.

"And that shame will feed me for decades."

A scream erupts from my throat as I cover my mouth and descend into blackness. The last thing I see is a wall of water, filled with fish and seaweed, rush toward El Cocodrilo as he disappears in a black fog.

TWENTY-THREE

A SOFT MELODY swirls over me, brushing my cheeks and pushing my hair out of my face. The slow notes rub my shoulders and pat my back.

I groan and open my eyes as Abuelita helps me sit up. Touching my face, I reach for my glasses.

"What happened?" I ask as I put my glasses on. "How'd I get home?"

Abuelita squeezes me in a hug as she sits next to me on my bed. "Te desmayaste en la escuela," she says.

I don't remember passing out at school. I squeeze my eyes shut as my skin shivers, remembering El Cocodrilo's glowing green eyes burning into mine.

Fautina sits on my other side. She reaches to take my hand but then clenches her fist and gives me a small smile instead.

"The school called here, and your abuelitos went and

picked you up. You were mumbling about flies the whole drive home," says a voice at the foot of the bed.

I adjust my glasses and see Pipo standing next to Abuelito. "You're here!" I exclaim.

Abuelito rubs his hands together. "Todavía es demasiado cobarde para competir conmigo."

"Listen, old man," Pipo says, elbowing his brother in the ribs even though his arm passes right through him. "You're too old to be climbing trees. Stop daring me to do it."

A grin breaks out on Abuelito's face, and he looks twenty years younger.

"¿Qué pasó, mi cielo?" Abuelita asks.

I sigh and put my head on Abuelita's shoulder. "It was El Cocodrilo. He said I'm ashamed of being Cuban. But I'm not. I'm really not."

"Are you sure about that?" a voice says from the corner of my room. My heart skips a beat as I hear the same question El Cocodrilo asked me in Principal Gearhart's office.

I look past Pipo and Abuelito to a girl standing next to a pile of clothes, water droplets falling from her skirt but disappearing before they reach my bedroom floor.

"Andaluz?"

Abuelita squeezes my hand and nods. "Ella está aquí para ayudarnos."

Andaluz shrugs. "Of course I have to help. It's not like you've been able to do anything yourself. Maybe if you weren't so embarrassed by your family."

I sit up straighter. "I'm really not. I promise. I get it now. I get why Abuelito and Abuelita have traditions to remind them of where they're from."

Andaluz rolls her eyes. "They've still forgotten a lot."

Abuelita's shoulders sag as she looks at Andaluz. "Lo siento, primita. Lo siento mucho."

"It's okay, Abuelita," I tell her. "I know you didn't forget Andaluz."

Andaluz crosses her arms and glares at me.

"I remember when I was in kindergarten," I say, "and you and Abuelito heard that Fidel Castro died. At first I didn't understand why you went out on our sidewalk and banged on pots and pans with wooden spoons. It was Peak Cubanity and super embarrassing. I didn't understand why you would celebrate someone dying, especially someone who was the leader of a country far away." I look directly at Andaluz. "But then I heard Abuelita praying. She prayed for peace for everyone she lost. Everyone Castro had taken from her . . . And she prayed for you. She remembered you."

Andaluz's face softens. Her dress glistens as the water droplets sparkle on it.

"And now that she's told me about you, I won't forget

either. I won't forget any of you," I say, looking at all my family, ghost and human, crammed in my small bedroom.

A knock on the door makes me jump, my muscles still tense.

"We came to make sure you were okay," Keisha says, followed closely by Juan Carlos.

"The school nurse said they found you on the floor of the principal's office," Juan Carlos says. "Principal Gearhart swears he never called you down to speak to him. And he's pretty ticked that his office got soaking wet for no reason. Not sure how that happened."

I look at Andaluz, and she winks.

"Well, your parents are on their way," Pipo says. "The school called them too. So maybe we should figure out what you're going to say to them. And how you're going to tell them about . . . this."

Pipo lifts his arm and slaps Abuelito on the back of the head, his hand passing right through Abuelito's skull. Abuelito turns and punches Pipo in the stomach, his fist disappearing in Pipo's belly.

Keisha's eyes grow wide as Juan Carlos whispers, "Awesome."

Abuelita shakes her head and then begins to usher our group to the kitchen table for a planning session fueled by the guava pastelitos she piled high on a plate and set between us.

Andaluz looks at the treats and says, "Those were always my favorite."

Pipo eyes the pastries and licks his lips. "I really wish I could still eat."

Abuelito grabs a pastelito and takes a large bite, letting the crumbs tumble on the front of his shirt. He winks at his brother, who promptly sticks his tongue out at Abuelito.

"Ay, Dios mío, es como tener dos niñitos," Abuelita says, rolling her eyes.

Keisha looks at me, and I point to my abuelito and tío abuelo. "My abuelita says they're like having two little boys."

We're so busy watching Abuelito and Pipo make fun of each other as Fautina conjures each of their ridiculous stories right in the kitchen that no one hears Mami and Papi come into the house.

"Mari! What happened?" Mami says, rushing to my side and examining my face. She presses the back of her hand to my forehead.

"I'm fine, Mami. Really," I say, brushing her hand aside.

"Are you sure, kiddo? The school secretary said they heard you scream and found you passed out," Papi says, putting his hand on my shoulder. "Sounds serious."

"I'm okay. The cafeteria lunches are . . . really something." I tug on the end of my Port Ballí Community College hoodie and look from Pipo to Fautina to Andaluz and then to my parents, biting my lip.

Mami finally looks away from me and turns to everyone seated at the table. She smiles at Keisha and Juan Carlos, saying, "Hey, Super Ojos. Thanks for coming over to check on Mari."

Her eyes fall on Fautina. "Hi," Mami says tentatively as she looks over to Pipo.

Papi looks from Pipo to Abuelito and back again. "Papi? Who's this?" he asks.

"Mi hermano," Abuelito replies.

Papi's eyes grow wide as he shakes his head. "Excuse me?"

"Papi, this is Pipo, Abuelito's brother," I say. "He's my tío abuelo and I guess your tío."

Juan Carlos slowly bites into a pastelito, watching Mami and Papi as the guava filling oozes out of the sides of the pastry.

"That's not funny, Mari," Papi says.

"What are you talking about?" Mami says. She looks at Pipo. "I'm sorry about that. Mari and her abuelo like to make up silly stories. So who are you?"

Pipo stands and brushes his hands on his pants. Squaring his shoulders, he says, "My name is Baldomero Feijoo. I'm Nano Feijoo's brother and your uncle."

Papi tries to speak, but his mouth just hangs open.

Mami finally says something. "But you're—"

"Dead?" Pipo says.

"Wh . . . what?" Papi stammers. "That's not possible."

"It's true," I say, walking over to Pipo, and he nods. We both hold our hands up as if to give each other a high five, except Pipo's hand passes right through my arm. I wiggle my fingers as my hand travels through Pipo's neck and out the other side of his body.

"What the—" Mami yells as she slaps her hand over her mouth. Papi stumbles into the chair I was sitting in.

Juan Carlos wads up the napkin Abuelita gave him and throws it at Pipo. It passes through his stomach and lands on the kitchen floor.

"Not helpful," Keisha whispers to him as Mami looks like she might pass out.

I turn to Fautina. "And this is Fautina Crespo. She's Abuelita's abuela."

Abuelita's eyes light up as she looks at her grandmother. Fautina smiles and nods. She watches Juan Carlos reach for Keisha's napkin and holds up a finger. Clicking her tongue, she says, "Don't you dare throw anything at me."

Instead, Juan Carlos hops up from his chair and lets Mami sit down. All the blood drains from her face as she looks from Pipo to Fautina. Papi rubs his temples with the tips of his fingers as he rests his elbows on the table.

I point to Andaluz, who's standing behind Abuelita and Fautina. "And this is Andaluz, Abuelita's cousin. She helped me today when I passed out in the office. She's really incredible."

Andaluz looks at me and smiles for the first time. I give her a wink and smile back. Her constantly wet hair and damp clothes aren't so frightening anymore.

Several moments pass in silence. My abuelitos and I shrug. Juan Carlos walks his fingers toward the plate of pastelitos, and Keisha slaps his hand. Pipo pokes his brother in the cheek, but his finger disappears two knuckles deep in Abuelito's face. Fautina tries to slap the table to get them to stop, but her hand passes directly through the wood. Andaluz gets bored and conjures up a small water spout in the palm of her hand, the water tornado dancing back and forth on her skin.

Mami takes it all in, her eyes the size of quarters. She looks like she might run straight for the bathroom at any moment.

Finally, Papi speaks up. "Okay, forgetting for a second the 'how,' would someone mind explaining to me the 'why'?"

I take a deep breath and wipe my hands on my jeans, readying myself to once again launch into the story of El Cocodrilo. I tell Mami and Papi about not burning the effigy on New Year's Eve and all the bad luck that followed. I tell them about Andaluz, Pipo, Fautina, and all the other dead relatives showing up to help because I wrote about them in the diary Abuelita gave me.

When I finish, I wait, staring at them.

Papi still has his head in his hands. His chest heaves, and he finally looks at me. "Is this why you keep jumping at things none of us are able to see?"

Juan Carlos nods. "That sounds about right."

Mami sighs. "And why you keep inspecting all the food Abuelita and I make? Like there's going to be something wrong with it?"

"That's definitely El Cocodrilo," Keisha says. "He's been making us as miserable as possible so he can feed off of our sadness."

"And you can make people appear out of thin air by writing about them? With *your* handwriting?" Papi asks, taking another deep breath.

"Hey, low blow," I shoot back. "But, yes. I can. It's pretty cool, really."

"So there's a plan for this El Cocodrilo guy? Something with . . . uh, dead relatives?" Mami asks. Papi puts his head in his hands again and exhales quickly.

Keisha speaks up. "Yes. We've got it all figured out. But we need Liset too. The more the better."

Mami raises her eyebrows. "Liset needs to know about all . . . this?" She gestures at Pipo and Fautina.

I nod. "Yep. I tried to capture El Cocodrilo with just me, Abuelito's mom—Migdalia—and Abuelita's cousin Ladislao, but it didn't work. There weren't enough of us to fight against him."

Papi groans, and I realize I've told him more about my adventures with ghost family members than he was probably ready to hear. "I'm gonna need some aspirin," he says. "Scratch that. I'm gonna need all the aspirin."

"Are you doing okay with all of this, Papi?" I ask.

Papi sighs as he rubs his temples again. "I'm just preparing for the monster headache Liset's reaction is most likely going to give me."

When Abuelita hands him the bottle of aspirin, he shakes out two tablets, looks at Andaluz, Pipo, and Fautina, and shakes out two more.

TWENTY-FOUR

OUR PLAN HAD been wrong this whole time.

One high-pitched scream from Liset would've driven El Cocodrilo away forever.

I explained El Cocodrilo's curse to her, as well as my ability to call up our ancestors by writing in the diary, but that's not what set her off. After Pipo and Abuelito had a kicking match in front of her, their legs flying through each other's shins, and Andaluz made water shoot from my ears, the scream that erupted from Liset's throat shook every window in the house.

I'd say Peak Cubanity, but I get it.

At least now we're ready.

When I mentioned that El Cocodrilo lost his scales and seemed to have more humanlike skin when I played "Guantanamera" at my audition, Abuelita suggested that some of our traditions could be used against him. I think she wanted an excuse to have a full-blown party, with all our favorite Cuban food. But she made us wait until Friday, insisting that we weren't allowed to have a party on a school night. I gave up trying to explain to her that El Cocodrilo's curse was worse than me falling asleep in math class.

Now, while Abuelita fries up thick slices of plantains to make tostones as Fautina and Migdalia watch, Mami stirs a large pot of garlicky frijoles negros, and I brush egg on the pastelito dough. Papi and Abuelito, under the direction of Pipo, are making lechón in the backyard.

I'm okay with this Peak Cubanity.

Just as I'm helping Mami add golden raisins and green olives to the seasoned ground beef simmering on the stove for picadillo, Keisha arrives, her fencing bag slung over her shoulder.

"Just in case." She winks. "So, you ready?"

I nod and pick up a large stuffed doll, practically the size of Ladislao, propped at the kitchen table. "Absolutely. Migdalia sewed a new effigy made from things we all gave her. This new one should be strong enough to catch him."

I hold up the effigy. The fabric on the head is sewn from pieces of my Houston Aeros hoodie, the fighter plane logo making a snarling face. The rest of the effigy is pieced together from the dress Mami wore on her first date with Papi—which she'd saved—as well as the baby dress Liset was baptized in and the tie Abuelito wore when he and Abuelita got married. It's stuffed with mango and avocado leaves and twigs from the backyard. Keisha glances over to where Migdalia is standing in the corner of the kitchen.

"You made this?" Keisha asks her. "It's amazing. Neither of my moms can sew at all."

Migdalia smiles and nods. "Thank you, my sweet. It's been fun to create for the family again."

Keisha helps Abuelita and Mami carry all the food out to the patio while I drag the large effigy to the bottom of the steps.

"Oh, that was my idea!" a voice shouts from the patio table. "I said bigger is always better!"

Ladislao jumps up and down, clapping and pointing to the effigy.

Liset sits next to him, her arms crossed, and rolls her eyes. "Why am I in charge of him again?" she asks.

Ladislao raises his hand and waves it furiously. "I know! Because I'm not supposed to get snot on the food!"

Liset huffs and blows her bangs off her forehead.

We all gather around the table, the smell of the food making my stomach growl. Before I can reach for a plate, Papi says, "Kiddo, why don't you run the plan by us again. Just so we can be sure how this is going to go."

I push up the sleeves of my hoodie. It doesn't matter that the mark on my arm shows. All the secrets are out.

"Well, assuming that my diary will conjure up *any* of our relatives, I'm going to write about El Cocodrilo, to force him to appear. Then I'll play "Guantanamera" on my violin—because reminding him of his past made him turn more human at my audition. Migdalia will get the effigy near him, so he'll be sucked into it. It should be strong enough to trap him now, because it's made of things that mean a lot to us. But y'all need to make sure we can get the effigy close. I know he'll be up to his usual tricks."

We dig in to the food, sharing stories and jokes, the sound carrying over the fence to Mykenzye's window. A light clicks on, and the curtains rustle.

My stomach does a little flop when I think she might be the audience for this showdown with El Cocodrilo, but I'll have to deal with that later.

"Super Ojos!" Juan Carlos shouts as he walks onto the patio. "Don't start without me!" He immediately eyes the food on the table and grins.

"This is the best boss battle ever. Guaranteed," he says, setting an overstuffed Señor Listopatodo next to his feet.

Fautina clears her throat. "I suppose we should begin."

Sitting next to Fautina, I open my diary. "I'm sorry to ask you to do this, because I know it might be painful. But could you tell me a memory you have of El Coco— . . . of Reinaldo? Your dad?"

Fautina thinks for a moment and sighs. "We remember the good with the bad, the sour with the sweet," she says, rubbing her temples and closing her eyes. "Reinaldo

Crespo—my father—visited the cemetery outside our town every year on July first."

As I write Fautina's words, the breeze in the yard picks up, rustling the leaves of the mango and avocado trees. I look up from the diary and squint at the grass.

Something is moving out there.

Fautina takes a deep breath. "I followed him one year and watched him place sprigs of butterfly jasmine on a grave. Did you know that's Cuba's national flower? My father would breathe in the scent of the jasmine and place it on the headstone. It was the only kind thing I ever saw him do."

I grip my pencil hard as three huge brown snakes slither between the blades of grass toward us. They raise their heads and hiss, their tongues flicking in and out. I scoot closer to Fautina as my heart races.

Juan Carlos jumps up behind me. "Keep writing. I've got this," he says, ripping open Señor Listopatodo and taking out a small brown glass bottle. He dumps the liquid in the bottle on a handful of wadded-up napkins.

The smell of spicy cinnamon wafts through the air as the snakes grow closer.

While I write Fautina's words, Juan Carlos hurls the napkins at the serpents. "Snakes hate certain smells," he says, "like cinnamon. Mom has a ton of these bottles at home. She thinks they'll keep me from getting a cold."

The snakes stop their advance in front of the cinnamon-soaked napkins. Pipo steps forward and wiggles his fingers, the sound of a flute floating on the breeze. The snakes raise their heads at the music. Moving toward the serpents, Pipo continues playing as his notes put them in a trance.

I glance at Mykenzye's window. Light seeps through a small crack between the curtains.

Pipo walks the hypnotized snakes back to the tree line as he waves his arms. I look around the yard.

"Anyone see him?" I ask.

Papi shakes his head. "Not yet, kiddo. We might need more in the diary."

Fautina takes a deep breath and continues. "One year, I stayed at the cemetery after he left. I crept up to the grave where he had laid the flowers and I read the headstone. It said Emilio Gonzalez Fabregát. He died on July first, 1898. He was the only person my father ever cared about, and he lost Emilio because he was ashamed of himself."

I think back to the story Fautina told about El Cocodrilo, about the man who died in his arms. All because he was trying to be someone he wasn't.

As I copy down what Fautina said, I hear a crack and snap in the yard. A rotten mango flies directly toward us and smashes at our feet, splattering juice on my jeans. Another crack pierces the air, and a blackened avocado rockets toward the patio and smacks the wooden steps next to me.

"Mari, back up!" Mami cries, pulling me off the steps by my arms.

Keisha pushes past me into the yard. "My turn," she says.

Another mango sails directly at her face, and she swings her fencing blade, knocking the overripe fruit to the ground. Maggots crawl from the splattered flesh. Juan Carlos rushes to her side, fishing rod in hand, and starts slashing at the rotten mangos and avocados hurling toward us.

"How long are we gonna have to do this? My arm is getting tired!" Juan Carlos shouts as he smacks an avocado with the reel of his fishing rod, green, slimy flesh splattering his shirt and glasses.

I glance quickly at Mykenzye's window and see her standing there, her mouth dropped open at the sight of the Super Ojos battling flying fruit in the yard.

Well, she's about to get a full show.

"Andaluz," I say as I huddle next to Mami. "It's your time to shine."

Andaluz hops up from her seat next to Liset and brushes her hands along the fabric of her skirt, water droplets falling on the patio.

"I was getting bored anyway," she says, winking at me.

Keisha grunts as she demolishes another mango right before it can hit Abuelito in the stomach. "Anytime you want to jump in is fine with me," she says to Andaluz.

The sound of rushing rain fills the yard, but no drops fall. A mango snaps off from the tree, but instead of hurtling toward Abuelita, it's doused by a sudden waterfall and rolls into a puddle that's formed in the grass. Andaluz smiles at me before she raises her arms and completely drenches the mango and avocado trees. The fruit falls to the ground, and a small river appears in the yard as she waves her fingers, carrying them away.

"That was awesome," Juan Carlos says. "I was getting tired of sword fighting guacamole."

"Me too," Keisha adds, giving Andaluz a thumbs-up.

Andaluz pushes her soaked hair out of her face and looks at Abuelita. "Don't forget that, Primita."

"Do you think I've told you enough?" Fautina asks me.

I look down at the diary. The words I've written about Reinaldo stretch and spread, thick black worms squirming across the page.

"This is it," I say. "He has to be coming."

From behind the dripping mango tree, a figure steps into the grass. His face is thin, cheekbones jutting through his skin. His hands shake as his nails dig into the trunk of the tree.

El Cocodrilo has arrived.

TWENTY-FIVE

A SANDAL FLIES past my ear and straight toward El Cocodrilo.

"¡Vete de aquí, mocoso!" Abuelita shrieks.

El Cocodrilo snarls as the sandal lands at his feet. The gray scales on his skin shine in the moonlight, and his eyes glow green.

"Phase two," I whisper to everyone. "We have to turn him human."

As if reading my mind, Abuelito hands me my violin and winks. Setting the diary down, I rest my instrument under my chin and begin to play "Guantanamera." The notes float around the yard. Abuelito and Migdalia clap their hands to the song, and soon their strong voices join my playing.

Pipo moves his fingers in the air, and a trumpet, marimba, and bongos join my violin. Papi gets up, grabs Mami's hand, and pulls her toward him, dancing to the song as they ignore El Cocodrilo seething and grunting over the music. Ladislao joins them, wiggling his hips and waving his arms. Fautina and Abuelita tap their feet to the rhythm of the song as Andaluz takes it all in, smiling softly.

El Cocodrilo spits on the ground and doubles over. His eyes turn from green to black abysses. The skin on his left cheek and right arm glistens as scales fall and reveal tan skin like mine.

I finish "Guantanamera" and look at Pipo. He rolls his shoulders and waves his arms. The opening notes of "La Bayamesa," the Cuban national anthem, swirl in the air. Abuelito clears his throat and begins to sing along. Soon, everyone has joined him.

El Cocodrilo claws at his face in frustration and crouches to the ground. He digs his hands into the dirt, his nails no longer green, but gray. He inches across the grass toward us, his chest heaving as spit flies from his mouth.

"Anything but that," he snarls. "Anything but that song."

Mami, Papi, and Andaluz form a wall in front of me as Keisha and Juan Carlos grip their weapons at the bottom of the patio stairs. Fautina stands next to me as my abuelitos and Pipo huddle beside us.

Migdalia waves her hand, and the effigy floats toward her. "My sweet, are you sure we can get close enough?" she asks Andaluz.

Andaluz shrugs. "This has already been a lot. We should

get rid of him the same way you made me disappear," she says to me.

I lower my violin as Pipo continues the song. "What do you mean?" I ask.

"My page in the diary got soaked, and I disappeared. Simple," Andaluz says with a smirk.

I think for a moment. El Cocodrilo sneers at us, his tongue darting in and out of his mouth as his black eyes glare at the effigy.

"I have an idea," I say. "Pipo, keep playing. Everybody sing along as much as you can. And Papi, I think it's time for some s'mores."

Papi looks at me, and then his eyes grow wide in realization. He gives me a thumbs-up and runs to the firepit, tossing in twigs and leaves.

The music swirling through the yard swells and El Cocodrilo pounds on the dirt with a clenched fist. Migdalia draws closer, and a crack fills the air as the wood on the patio begins to splinter. Liset shrieks as a board next to her splits apart. Ladislao lets out a forceful sneeze, securing the board back together with a thick layer of slime.

El Cocodrilo snarls and slithers closer to us. Keisha swings her fencing blade in his direction, and he gnashes his teeth at her. His skin is completely free of scales, and his eyes are now golden brown, just like Abuelita's and mine.

"Stop—" he gasps, his chest heaving. His eyes snap to

Fautina. "How dare you tell them about . . . about him. How dare you use that against me."

He slashes at the ground, dirt pushing under his jagged nails. He spits as he inches toward Juan Carlos, baring his teeth and snarling.

I have an idea, and I set my violin down, snatching my diary off the table. I rip out the page where I wrote about Reinaldo, the words now completely obscured, shaped like fat worms that have been smashed between the pages, their guts smeared across the paper. Running over to Migdalia, I hold out the page.

"Can you sew this inside? I think it will make it easier to trap him. His story has power over him," I tell her.

Migdalia winks and waves her hand. A small thread comes loose on the side of the effigy, and I tuck the page inside. Migdalia snaps her fingers and the seam closes again.

I cross the yard and stand in front of El Cocodrilo, my stomach rolling at being so close to him. Keisha, Juan Carlos, and Andaluz are behind me, and I can hear Juan Carlos's shaky breathing.

"We've got you, Mari," Keisha says.

"I'd love to see him try anything," Andaluz says, smirking.

El Cocodrilo slams his hand on the ground, and thick black cockroaches squirm out from the dirt beneath his palm, their spiny legs stumbling over the blades of grass. I step forward and squash one with my shoe.

"You can't make me feel ashamed anymore. It won't work. You know why?" I say as I spot Papi lighting the twigs in the firepit with a match. "I know who I am and who my family is. And I'm proud of it."

El Cocodrilo groans in pain as he writhes in the dirt, his black, stringy hair hanging in front of his face. His chest shudders as he sucks in a breath. "You can't have it all. You have to pick. They'll make you." He spits. "And if you don't choose correctly, you won't belong anywhere. No one will accept you."

I clench my fists. "Sure, there will always be ignorant people."

Glancing next door at Mykenzye's window, I spot her staring at me and the chaos in the backyard.

I shake my head. "What other people think about me is never going to take anything away from who I really am. I'm Maricela Yanet Feijoo. I don't have to pick what side of me to show, because all of it makes me who I am. I'm proud of every single part."

I walk toward the firepit, the flames dancing high, and hold the effigy over the heat.

As his eyes dart from the effigy to me, El Cocodrilo screams and reaches out a gangly arm, its skin sagging.

"I'm not ashamed of who I am," I say. "And I'm not scared of you."

I drop the effigy into the firepit as El Cocodrilo pounds

the ground with his fists. Thick black smoke rises from the flames as the effigy, with the page inside, is consumed. The dark cloud floats toward El Cocodrilo as he sneers and scowls.

Keisha and Juan Carlos hold out their shaky weapons toward him as black tendrils from the smoke wrap around El Cocodrilo's torso. They squeeze his body, dark veins popping from his neck and arms. He opens his mouth to scream, but the smoke cloud slithers down his throat and chokes him.

I stand in front of El Cocodrilo again, and Fautina appears beside me.

"Goodbye, Papi," she says.

The black fog covers El Cocodrilo, and his body disappears in the smoke. A final scream pierces my ears, and I gasp as the mark on my arm burns.

I look at Keisha. She is holding her arm to her chest, her hand wrapped around her skin as she winces.

Slowly, the thick smoke fades and floats up to the sky, disappearing and taking the ashes of what was El Cocodrilo with it.

I tug the sleeve of my hoodie, revealing clear skin. The mark is gone.

A whoop and holler from Abuelito breaks the silence, and everyone shouts and claps.

Looking up at the window next door, I see Mykenzye still staring at me.

Squaring my shoulders and facing her, I shout, "Peak Cubanity!" and take a bow.

▼△▽△▽△▽△▽△▽△▽△▼

TWENTY-SIX

⌒ FAUTINA ⌒

WE SIT HUDDLED on a wooden bench overlooking the fishing pier in Port Ballí—my dear niece Andaluz and cousin Ladislao as well as Pipo and Migdalia. The sea breeze rustles the palm fronds and the feathers of the laughing gulls searching for crabs on the beach, but it leaves our hair unbothered. My long purple skirt hangs still, despite the wind picking up and filling the air with the smell of salt.

We watch Mari walk to the middle of the pier, a rectangular black case in her hand. She's accompanied by Keisha and Juan Carlos as well as by another boy, each carrying fishing poles. Juan Carlos hands the boy a pair of orange-framed glasses, and they all laugh when he puts them on and wiggles his eyebrows. While they ready their bait to entice the schools of flounder and pinfish circling in the water, Mari takes out a violin from her case and adjusts the strings.

"I wanna fish too!" Ladislao says, clapping.

I put my finger to my lips and shush him. "Leave them be. We'll just watch."

Pipo smiles and twirls his fingers in the air, a soft melody floating on the breeze to the beat of his tapping foot.

Migdalia chuckles. "Just listen. Let her play."

As Keisha, Juan Carlos, and the other boy toss their fishing lines into the water, Mari begins to play a lively song, the notes dancing down the wooden planks of the pier, across the sand, and around us on the bench. I close my eyes and take a deep breath, listening to the music.

Mari sways back and forth as she plays the song. When it ends, the smattering of people who are fishing on the pier clap. One man, wearing a Port Ballí Middle School baseball cap, approaches her and pats her on the shoulder. As they chat, Mari smiles broadly.

"Looks like someone's getting another chance to try out for mariachi," Andaluz says.

"Now that all that bad luck nonsense is over, I know she'll do much better," Pipo replies. "She's not the only one who got a second chance."

I nod and look at Keisha, spinning around to show off her jacket with "Houston Daggers" embroidered on the back.

As Migdalia and Ladislao sit next to me, their feet slowly fade, the cracked sidewalk visible beneath them. I examine my own hands and see the purple threads of my skirt through my red nails.

"We won't be here much longer, will we?" Ladislao asks, staring at the kids on the pier, memorizing every detail.

I shake my head as Migdalia's gray hair fades in the setting sun. "I don't believe so. But it's for the best, isn't it? We did our part, and now it's time to go back," I say.

Pipo grips the fabric on his pants, as if hanging on to himself might make him remain on the beach a little longer. "I wish we had more time. I always seem to want more time," he says, his voice catching in his throat. He starts to rise from the bench, but Migdalia stops him.

"Leave them be. They've already said their goodbyes. They don't need to see us disappear," she says.

Pipo's shoulders slump. The fabric of his pants slowly fades into the wooden slats of the bench.

Andaluz waves her hand, and a small wave moves unnaturally against the tide and toward Juan Carlos standing on the pier. He pulls on his fishing pole, jumping up and down as he reels in a silvery brown striped pinfish. Mari, Keisha, and the other boy slap him on the back and give him high fives.

"You cheated," Ladislao tells Andaluz, winking.

She shrugs and smiles.

I clear my throat as the purple of my skirt lightens and dissolves in the air. "We'll always be here, you know. In our own way."

Pipo looks at me, his eyebrows knitted in confusion. His dark brown hair dims and dulls as it becomes transparent.

"Every time Mari plays a song, you'll be there," I say. "Every time she tells a story, I'll be there. Every time she does something brave or silly, Migdalia and Ladislao will be there. Every time she stands up for herself, Andaluz will be there. We may not be walking around, breathing their air, but we'll remain. We'll be remembered."

Pipo takes a deep breath. His torso fades into the bench, and he gives me one last look. "I suppose that's enough. Don't you think so, Mami?"

Migdalia nods and smiles as her pale green dress fades into the air and she disappears.

Ladislao chuckles and waves furiously at the Super Ojos standing on the pier. But it's too late. His arms turn to mist, and the breeze catches his form, sending it away in the air.

Andaluz stands and brushes her hands on her blue skirt. "I guess it's time to go, isn't it?" she asks.

Slowly, she walks barefoot across the sand to the edge of the water. A small wave laps at her feet, but before it retreats, she's gone, carried by the tide.

I reach for Pipo's hand, but it's already vanished. Looking down, I see my own arm slowly disappearing.

"Goodbye, Fautina," Pipo says, his sparkling brown eyes vanishing in the setting sun until he's completely gone.

"Goodbye, Pipo," I say to the sea breeze.

I look one last time at the Super Ojos on the pier. Their laughter carries over the crashing waves as they fling their fishing lines into the water again.

But Mari lifts her head to the wind coming off the waves, closing her eyes and breathing in the salty air.

As if sensing something she knows is there but can't quite find, she gazes up and down the beach, past skittering crabs and prowling shorebirds.

Until she finds me.

Her eyes fall on my fading form, and she lifts her hand in a small wave. I want to wave back, to say goodbye to my great-great-granddaughter, but all she would see is the clump of tangled cordgrass behind me.

The pull in my stomach taking me away from the beach grows, and I smile at Mari as the wind plays in her dark brown hair. She nods and turns away from me and back to her friends as they point to the schools of fish darting in the water.

And in the next moment, I fade and am gone, only a memory in the minds of those I leave behind, only a name in a family tree.

And that's how I'll stay.

Until another story is written down, another memory is passed from parent to child, words in a never-ending book telling the tales of those who remain in our hearts.

AUTHOR'S NOTE

New Year's traditions are as varied in Latin America as its people. Even within one country, practices change from house to house, just as they do in the United States. As a result, one can't say with confidence, "This is how Cubans celebrate the new year."

Growing up, my family celebrated with a whole roasted hog, fireworks, and the Miami Orange Bowl parade. We didn't burn effigies, our fear of setting our house on fire overriding any superstitions.

The practice of burning an effigy isn't unique to Cuba. Large stuffed scarecrows called años viejos are burned in Mexico and Colombia, as well as other countries. Sometimes the scarecrow is even stuffed with fireworks.

Other common and popular Cuban traditions are rooted in superstition. For example, if you want to get rid of bad luck and start over on January first, burning an effigy isn't your only option. A safer (and nonflammable) choice would be to sweep and mop your entire house, throwing the dirty water out your door at midnight. If you want to travel in the new year, walk around your block holding a suitcase. You could also try eating twelve grapes at midnight. Each grape represents a month of the year, and you make a wish as you eat each one. Just be sure you don't choke!

Finally, a word on Mari and her abuelos. The way they communicate, with Mari speaking English and her abuelos speaking Spanish, mirrors the way I grew up talking to my own abuelos. When learning a new language, receptive language (listening and reading) is learned before productive language (speaking and writing). Many multilingual families with different levels of language acquisition often communicate this way.

ACKNOWLEDGMENTS

As an introvert, I'm happy creating my books in the solitude of my living room, accompanied only by my cat and dog. But in reality no book is created by just one person. It takes a team of amazing individuals to put a story in readers' hands. Each and every one of them deserves the largest plate of pastelitos.

My agent, Stefanie Von Borstel of Full Circle Literary, deserves the highest praise for helping me break out of my shell and attempt things I never thought possible.

Many thanks to editor Carolina Ortiz for seeing the heart of this story and guiding me as I revised it over . . . and over . . . and over. Thank you to artist Valentino Lasso for creating the cover of my dreams!

I am forever grateful for my support group of amazing individuals who cheer me on, listen to me vent, and let me be exactly who I am—Amparo, Natalia, Lori, Yaikira, Ceci, and Minh.

To the amazing young readers I meet at school visits, thank you for inspiring me each time I sit down to write. I always picture your excited faces as we gush about stories, marvel at our magnificent brains, and laugh at heroes making terrible choices.

Finally, to my husband, Joe, and my son, Soren. You are the brightest parts of my life and I wouldn't be able to tell the stories I do without you by my side. Thank you for your constant love, support, and bonkers ideas that will most likely never see the page.

The author marching in the Miami Orange Bowl parade as a child.

Voluntarily . . . not because she was cursed by El Cocodrilo.